THE GREEN LADY

by

Lisa Picard

Me 'n My Dog
Publishers

ME 'N MY DOG PUBLISHERS

Published by
Me 'n My Dog Publishers
PO Box 2100, Knysna, 6570, South Africa

First published in both e-book and paperback formats
by Me 'n My Dog Publishers, 2015
(version 1.3)

Printed by Lightning Source

ISBN: 978-0-620-67629-8

CONTENTS

Contents

For Arn, who has always encouraged me to go to my heart to find the magic and wonder within.

"And, above all, watch with glittering eyes the whole world around you because the greatest secrets are always hidden in the most unlikely places. Those who don't believe in magic will never find it."
Roald Dahl

South Africa's Garden Route

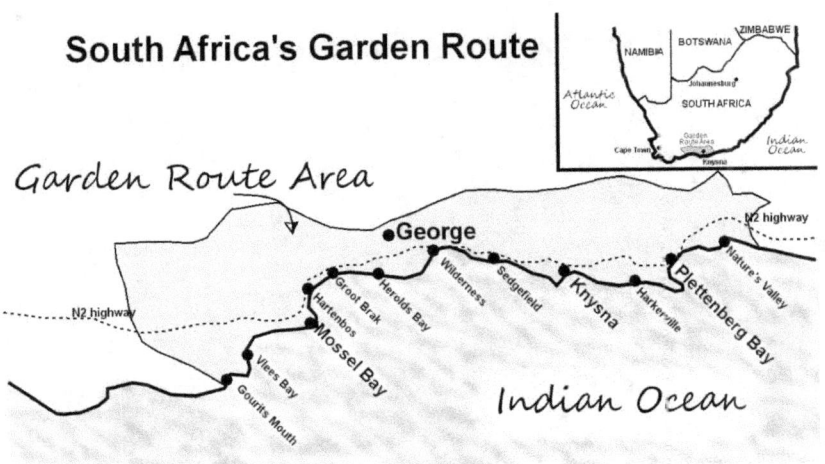

The Forests of the Knysna Area

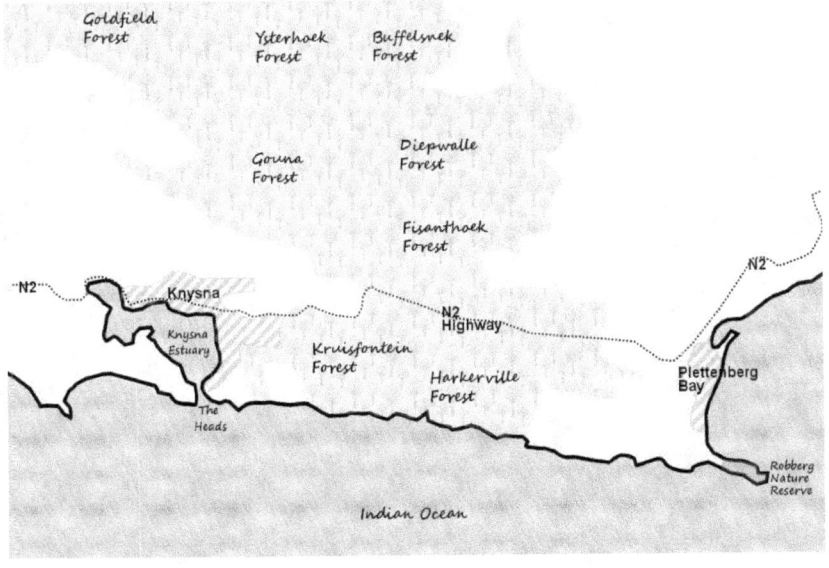

Chapter 1
The Genesis of the Book

In the spring of the year I turned forty, my perfectly comfortable, predictable and well-ordered life began to fall apart.

It all started when Clare, my girlfriend of five years, uttered those four dreaded words, which strike terror into the heart of the bravest man.

"*Peter, we need to talk,*" she told me, her warm, brown eyes that normally brimmed over with good humour regarding me now with the utmost gravity. It turned out that she had decided to leave me. She would be departing on a month-long backpacking vacation across Europe with a girlfriend within two weeks and she made it very clear that, when she returned, she expected me to have vacated our shared home.

There was very little anger or acrimony involved; it was simply that Clare and I clearly wanted different things in life. She had recently turned thirty-five and had finally given up on trying to change my mind about having children (she wanted them and I didn't) and marriage, an institution to which I, as the son of a thrice-divorced mother, was not favourably disposed. Clare's wealthy grandmother had died six months earlier, leaving her with a considerable inheritance, with which she proposed to pay me, at a market-related price, for my half of our shared house. Clare was always scrupulously fair and honest to a fault. I didn't actually object to this proposal, as the house had always been more to Clare's taste than mine, and I certainly didn't relish the thought of having to manage on my own the housework and upkeep required by such a large place. However, it did mean that I would need to find alternate accommodation, and fast. I mused sadly to myself that, in a way, it was almost a blessing that my beloved Golden Retriever, Max, had moved on to greener pastures a couple of months earlier. I was aware that the absence of a large, hairy, ancient and very smelly dog would considerably simplify my search for a new, short-term rental.

And the changes didn't stop with my home situation. My career was about to undergo a radical change as well.

I had been working since my graduation from university some fifteen years earlier as a journalist for a top daily newspaper in Cape Town. I had, over the years, developed somewhat of a reputation for my tenacity and my ability to always "get the story". But lately I had started to lose my edge. Somewhat to my dismay, I realised that I wasn't quite as hungry for the story anymore. The daily news had begun to feel rather tediously rinse-repeat to me and my energy and enthusiasm were definitely on the wane. It was becoming very clear to me that I needed to pull it together fast or I would rapidly become victim to the ruthless ambitions of younger, hungrier journalists fighting for opportunities to make their mark.

In addition to these changes, my best friend and pub-buddy of some ten years, Mark, his wife and two children had packed for Perth three months earlier. Mark and his wife believed that they would be able to secure a better future for their children in Australia. With gregarious and sociable Mark's departure, our small circle of friends seemed to lose their glue and we gradually drifted apart. For the first time in years, I found my previously busy social life to have become somewhat quiet and I was secretly relishing the time and space now available to consider my future

One Saturday morning, a few days after Clare's departure, and with no action yet taken to resolve either my home- or work-related dilemmas, I was awoken before dawn by the barking of the neighbour's dog. Rather than turning over and going back to sleep, I decided to get up instead and go for a hike on Table Mountain, in an attempt to clear my head. I decided to hike from the Kirstenbosch Botanical Gardens up Skeleton Gorge, a beautiful, forested ravine on Table Mountain, and then take Smuts Track all the way to Maclear's Beacon, the highest point on the mountain at 1,086 meters. Although relatively strenuous, this remains one of my favourite hikes up the mountain, as it allows one to experience the dense Afro-montane forest in the ravine, as well as all the floral zones on the mountain and some truly spectacular views over False Bay and the vineyards of Constantia Valley, all the way to the Hottentot Holland Mountains in the distance.

By six-thirty I was already in the ravine and I kept up a steady pace to emerge onto Smuts Track less than an hour later. This popular track was named after Jan Smuts, a South African statesman, philosopher, author and keen hiker, who reportedly hiked this route regularly, well into his eighties. I maintained my pace and emerged onto the Table Mountain Plateau, stopping for a well-deserved water break and breather. I spent some time admiring the beautiful flowering fynbos[1], a floral biome unique to South Africa's Western Cape Province, before setting off to Maclear's Beacon.

---

1   Translates to "fine bush" in English. Fynbos is a collective term for thousands of flowering plants, indigenous to the unique Cape floral biome of South Africa.

I had not encountered a single other hiker on the trail thus far, but as I stowed my water bottle in preparation for continuing the walk, a soft voice to my right disrupted my reverie.

"Beautiful day for a hike, isn't it?" Startled, I whipped around to find a dapper and dignified-looking elderly man with a neat and well-trimmed white beard and clear blue eyes, leaning on a wooden walking stick and gently smiling at me.

"Goodness!" I exclaimed, *"I didn't see you. How long have you been here?"*

He disregarded my question, suggesting instead, *"Shall we walk together?"* and then setting off at a spanking pace on the path to the beacon. I shrugged and followed him.

Shortly afterwards I found that I was thoroughly enjoying myself. My companion was excellent company and provided a wealth of interesting information on the plants and birdlife of the mountain. He also had a delightful, dry wit, which had me chuckling out loud on several occasions. I realized that I had been feeling rather lonely and melancholy on the first part of the hike and that I was now having a lot more fun. I found myself telling the old man about the recent events in my life, which was rather unusual for me, as I was normally the one coaxing the story out of someone else. But it was very easy to talk to my companion, whom I experienced as an excellent, non-judgmental listener, who was also rather astute in his comments.

Once we had reached Maclear's Beacon, we stood for some time admiring the breathtaking views over the whole of Table Mountain, all the way to Cape Point, Table Bay, Devil's Peak and Robben Island where Nelson Mandela had been incarcerated for eighteen years. The old man turned to me, fixing me with his intense blue gaze, and then said something which caused a chill to run down my spine. *"The art of life is all about timing, my young friend. You need to pay attention to the signs guiding you to where you next need to go. It seems to me that life is telling you that it's time to take that leap. What are you waiting for?"*

Wordlessly, I stared at him for a few moments, before the screech of an eagle high above us caught my attention and I briefly glanced up to see if I could catch a glimpse of the bird. When I looked back at my companion again, he had simply disappeared! Gone. Not a sign of him anywhere, as far as the eye could see!

"Hello? Hello? Where have you gone?" I called, over-and-over-again but there was no response whatsoever and it was very clear to me that there was absolutely nowhere to hide on the rocky plateau of the mountain.

Thoroughly spooked, I collapsed onto a large rock, my legs no longer able to support my weight. I repeatedly shook my head, simply unable to believe the evidence supplied by my eyes. What had just happened? Who had the old gentleman been? Had it all just been an hallucination? But, no! He had been just as real as I was, of that I was convinced. But, then... where had he gone?

But, very gradually, an overwhelming sense of gratitude started to swell in my heart, and tears began to squeeze past the constriction in my throat to well up in my eyes. Did it really matter who he had been? He had provided me with exactly what I had needed, when I most needed it. Surely this was one of those signs that were pointing me in the direction I next needed to go? The more I thought about it, the more I realized that I knew exactly what it was that I wanted to do. An idea that had been slowly germinating in my subconscious for several months suddenly blossomed into my full consciousness and I was overwhelmed by a bubbling sense of excitement and anticipation.

The very next day I approached my editor with the idea of taking a six-month sabbatical from my job. I knew that this was tantamount to career suicide in the fast-moving journalistic world, but I guess that I wasn't ready to completely sever myself from my familiar world by resigning just yet. The fact that it was surprisingly easy to convince my editor was further confirmation for me that my career had been on a downturn. I also knew that, if I was to return six months later, I would need to put in a concerted effort into putting my career back on track. Despite the panic-inducing potential of this thought, I felt remarkably light-hearted, happy and sure of my decision. A month later, I packed my pathetically few personal possessions into a cardboard box and departed from the offices in which I had spent the better part of fifteen years.

Over the next few weeks I boxed up and donated the majority of my belongings to several local charities and rented a container in which I stashed the few remaining items. I completed the outstanding necessary administrative duties and then packed a single suitcase and my laptop into my battered old Fiat station wagon. I drove the 550km to the small coastal town of Knysna, singing along to an old 80's rock album, feeling younger and more optimistic than I had felt in years.

Once I arrived in Knysna, I rapidly found a small, furnished apartment in town at an affordable price. Within hours I had unpacked my few bits of clothing into the wardrobe, set up my laptop and stocked the refrigerator and cupboards with some basic groceries. I sank down onto the couch and released years of pent-up frustration and unfulfilled desires, of which I had up till this point been unaware, in a prolonged, very loud, heartfelt sigh of contentment. My entire body thrummed with excitement and I inwardly beamed as I realized that I was now finally ready for my new life to begin.

So, having kept you in suspense thus far, I guess it's time to tell what my idea was all about. Several months prior to the events described above, Clare and I had been holidaying in a self-catering cottage in Knysna. As I waited for Clare to get ready for a forest hike we had planned, I picked up, and began reading, a small booklet on the hikes in Knysna and the surrounding areas. A humorous footnote at the bottom of a description of a hike into ancient, untouched, indigenous forest informed me that, *"Over the years many hikers, forestry workers and local inhabitants have described encounters they have had with a so-called spirit of the forest. Apparently, this Green Lady appears at moments of deep personal transformation and seems to have a positive effect on most of those who encounter her. But, woe betide those seeking to harm the forest or her creatures! The Green Lady can be a serious adversary to those of ill intent."*

The tiny seed of an idea that had been planted by the footnote described above was further nurtured by an event that occurred a few months later. Whilst I was waiting for a colleague to return to his office, I picked up a newspaper lying on his desk and idly paged through it. It was the local Knysna newspaper, The CX Express, which he had brought back with him to Cape Town after a recent visit to the Garden Route. An article written by Helena Kroukamp, a free-lance journalist living in Knysna, caught my eye. It was a whimsical, tongue-in-cheek piece about the abundance of supernatural experiences to be had in the forests of Knysna. Somehow this article sparked my imagination.

I had always held in the back of my mind the intent to write a novel (don't we all!) My encounter with the old gentleman on the top of Table Mountain and the two events described above had provided me with the idea for a book. I would spend my six-month sabbatical in Knysna, using my journalistic skills to find, and interview, those who had experienced supernatural encounters in the forests of the region. I would use the material thus obtained as the basis for my first novel. I had always believed that Knysna had many secret stories just waiting to be told and so I decided that I would be the one to tell them!

Before I left for Knysna, I did some research about the town so as to prepare myself for my work there. Below is a very short summary of what I found.

The charming coastal town of Knysna, in the heart of South Africa's beautiful Garden Route, is a favourite tourist destination. Knysna lies thirty-four degrees south of the equator, between the Indian Ocean and the Outeniqua Mountains, which are covered by indigenous vegetation. Dramatic sandstone cliffs, the Knysna Heads, separate the warm water estuary from the ocean. This estuary, which is fed by the Knysna River, is a protected marine reserve and home to the endangered seahorse and over two hundred species of fish. South Africa's largest Afro-montane or temperate, lush, indigenous, closed-canopy forests can be found in-and-around Knysna. These forests, which were made famous by Dalene Matthee's book, *Circles in the Forest*, are home to Africa's most southern, and only free roaming, elephant herd.

The Knysna area, with its oceanic climate, has one of the highest rainfalls in South Africa and is green all year round. Higher up in the Outeniqua Mountains, the beautiful and remarkably diverse fynbos contributes over eight thousand plant species to the Cape floral kingdom.

Knysna and the surrounding areas offer wild pristine beaches, large lakes, breathtaking views and countless hiking trails. The area is on the migratory route of southern right whales, other whale species and dolphins. It is also home to several seal colonies.

The wild, unspoiled beauty of the area encourages creativity and therefore Knysna provides sanctuary to vast numbers of artists, healers, as well as interesting eccentrics of every kind.

Chapter 2
The Lady

When I first arrived in Knysna I knew absolutely no-one in the town and I was somewhat challenged as to how I would go about finding the stories that I required for my book. I tried a number of different approaches, one of which was to place an advertisement in the Action Ads, a weekly publication of classified advertisements, which is freely available just about everywhere in Knysna. My ad read:

Have YOU had a supernatural encounter
in the Knysna forests?
TELL ME YOUR STORY
It could possibly be included in a book!

As it turned out, I received only one positive response to my advertisement, but it did lead to the very first story of this book.

I was contacted by a middle-aged woman called Evie. She told me that she had lived next door to a lovely old lady, named Lucy Baldwin, whilst growing up. Lucy and Evie, despite the large age gap, became firm friends and Evie would spend Saturday afternoons with the delightfully eccentric old woman, baking cookies, doing art projects or simply chatting. Lucy shared with Evie the story of her life and her several encounters with the Lady, as she called her, during these Saturday afternoon visits.

The first part of the tale below is based upon Evie's memories of the stories that Lucy had shared with her over the years. The final part of Lucy's story was purely a product of Evie's imagination, but I liked it so much that I decided to include it in my book. When I tried to pay Evie for the story, she refused, saying, *"It's not my story, but Lucy's. But I know that she would have loved to have had it included in your book. So please do use it and do her proud. This is my way of remembering a lovely old lady and a wonderful friend, who was such a positive influence in my life."* This, then, is Lucy's story.

The first time Lucy saw the Lady she was only four years old. Although the house was full of people murmuring in hushed tones over endless cups of cooling tea and fishpaste sandwiches with curled-up edges, nobody noticed Lucy slipping away through the kitchen door and tip-toeing down the weed-choked garden path. At the bottom of the garden the overgrown honeysuckle bush hid from sight the loose board in the fence that Lucy had discovered a week earlier when she had been banished outdoors whilst the grown-ups whispered with furrowed brows and furtive tears. The little girl slipped behind the honeysuckle bush and crawled through the gap in the fence, allowing the loose board to swing back into place behind her.

Lucy found herself in a bramble- and nettle-infested tangle; the wild grasses tickling her snub little nose as, for a moment; she experienced the thrill of her very first foray into illicit territory. Her mother had strictly forbidden her from venturing alone into the wild and forested area behind the house. A wave of sadness washed over Lucy as she remembered that her mother would never again forbid her to do anything and she stood in the sunshine, her bottom lip quivering as she gulped back tears whilst rubbing her eyes with her fists. She had never felt so alone in her entire short life. Just then, she was momentarily distracted from her sorrow by a sudden cacophonous chirruping, as a large flock of Cape White Eyes swooped right past her and into the thick forested area a few meters ahead. Looking around, Lucy noticed a narrow animal path stretching ahead through the brambles into the tangled thicket beneath the trees and, without a moment's thought to the consequences of her actions, she set off down the path.

The tangled undergrowth was extremely dense, but the child was small and the spirit of adventure driving her progress was a welcome respite from her sadness as she burrowed along the animal track. After a while, the path broke through into a small clearing under the canopy of massive trees and Lucy looked around, trying to locate the way forward. She might have turned back at this point, as she suddenly remembered her parents' warnings about the dangers of children getting lost in the forest, but then a beautiful, large, white butterfly fluttered past and disappeared between the trees and, without a second's thought, Lucy ran after it, winding between the trees and crawling under brush in her attempts to keep the butterfly in sight.

After a short while Lucy lost sight of the butterfly, but now her attention was attracted by the brilliant orange bracket fungi growing on a dead tree up ahead, and so she meandered through the forest, her attention constantly diverted by some wonder or another. After about an hour, Lucy's steps began to slow down and she became aware of the fact that she was tired and thirsty, not to mention, extremely hungry. She remembered that she hadn't eaten any lunch and that she had only managed a few spoonfuls of cereal that morning; her father and aunt being far too distracted by all the funeral arrangements to notice. She also started to feel a little bit scared because she couldn't remember how she had gotten to where she now found herself. When she also remembered that nobody knew that she had gone exploring, Lucy's lower lip started to quiver and she whispered, "*Mommy, mommy...* *Where are you?*" her voice rising in agitation at the end of the sentence, as she remembered that her mommy had gone to heaven and that she wouldn't be back again, ever. Now Lucy started to bawl in earnest; the intrepid adventurer giving way to a scared, lonely and lost little girl.

Suddenly there was a loud crashing in the trees above and a harsh, grating, cawing sound sent Lucy running for the relative safety of a nearby Yellowwood tree, where she crouched amongst the massive roots, hiding her face in her hands, her little heart wildly fluttering as she whimpered in fear.

After a while the realization gradually dawned upon Lucy that everything had become extremely quiet and she dared to peep through her fingers to check if she was safe. Lowering her hands, she gasped in surprise, as she noticed that the entire clearing was suffused in a softly glowing, green light. And, drifting through the light towards the little girl was the most beautiful Lady that she had ever seen. The Lady was very tall and slender, with pale green, luminous skin and long, tangled, dark-green hair, adorned with lichen, ferns and bits of bark. Although the Lady was clothed only in soft green light, it was the most beautiful raiment that Lucy had ever seen. As she stared in fascination, a small lizard crawled up the Lady's arm and disappeared into her hair and two little birds landed on her outstretched hand, briefly preening before fluttering away into the treetops.

"*Who... who are you?*" whispered Lucy, who had completely forgotten her fear and sadness in her wonderment at the vision standing before her. The Lady gently smiled and came to a stop right in front of the tree under which Lucy was sheltering.

Lucy heard the Lady's answer in her heart, "*I am the Deva, the spirit who takes care of this forest. I think that perhaps you may be lost?*" At that, Lucy remembered her plight and tears once more began to run down her cheeks. The Lady reached out a hand and, with one long, slender finger, she gathered Lucy's teardrops, which rolled down into her hand, one-by-one. With her other hand she reached out and gently unwound a long, shimmering piece of silk from a spider web just above Lucy's head. Then, with a few deft movements of her long, graceful hands, she threaded the teardrops onto the spider silk and tied the ends together behind her neck. Lucy forgot to cry as she stared in admiration at the exquisitely beautiful, iridescent teardrops sparkling against the Lady's glowing green skin.

Then the Lady lifted her chin and made a soft, gentle sound like the wood pigeons that Lucy had often heard in the woodpile behind the cottage. "*Coerrrr...*" and Lucy gasped in amazement as the sound emerging from the Lady's mouth transformed into a delicate white flower, which the Lady plucked from the air and dropped into Lucy's lap. "*Coerrrr.... coerrr... coerrr...*" went the Lady until Lucy's lap was filled with fragrant white flowers. Then Lucy's strange companion plucked a long, green hair from her head and twined it through the flower stems, fashioning a beautiful crown of flowers, which, with the sweetest smile imaginable, she placed upon Lucy's head.

The Lady stretched out her hand and, without a moment's hesitation, despite all the warnings she had received about being wary of strangers, Lucy took the proffered hand and followed the Lady into the forest, feeling like a fairy princess with her crown of flowers. Everything looked different too, in the gentle green glow emitted by the Lady and now Lucy could see all kinds of forest animals, birds and reptiles and the plant life surrounding them, shimmering with energy and life. She could actually see the trees growing and breathing and every leaf, flower and twig was tended to by tiny, magical, fairylike creatures.

*"Those are the sylphs, air elementals who look after the plants and make sure that they grow and flower, "*the Deva whispered deep into Lucy's heart. Lucy's attention was captured by a fiery flash, as a small, lizard-like creature dashed across her path into the undergrowth. *"That was a salamander, an earth elemental, responsible for the transformation of dead plant material into nutrients to support the growth of new plants,"* the Lady informed Lucy. Lucy was absolutely enchanted; she had only ever heard about such mystical beings in the stories that her parents had read to her at bedtime. A whole new magical world was being revealed to her by her new friend.

"I need to take you back home now," the Deva said to Lucy, *"Your family will be worried about you."*

"But, I'd rather stay here with you," Lucy protested.

"You can always come and visit the forest, little one," smiled the Lady. *"Walk into the forest with an open heart and you will find that the most wondrous experiences will always*

await you." With that, she took Lucy's hand again and they turned to go home. Although Lucy had been wandering deeper and deeper into the forest for quite some time earlier, it was only a matter of minutes before she was right back in the bramble-infested clearing, just outside her garden fence. The Lady kissed her on her forehead and a warm, gentle glow filled Lucy's being as she pushed aside the loose plank and waved to the Lady before entering once more into her normal world.

For months thereafter Lucy would often slip through the fence and follow the animal track into the forest where she would spend hours calling for the Lady, but she was not to see her again for many years. However, her interest in the plants and animals of the forest, which had been awakened by her interaction with the Lady, grew steadily. She started to pay more attention to the forest around her and later, when she learned to read, she began to identify the names of the trees and plants that she encountered. This was to become her lifelong passion and, eventually, her livelihood. At first Lucy's father was worried that she would get lost in the forest, but gradually he realized that she was perfectly fine on her own and eventually he capitulated to the inevitable and built a small gate in the fence so that Lucy could come and go at will.

After the death of her mother, Lucy's father became silent and withdrawn. He spent most of his time in the spare bedroom, which he had converted into a study for himself, doing the translations that earned their keep, and latterly, doing online research for, and writing, the historical novels which would gradually become their sole source of income. Lucy knew that her father loved her, but he lived inside his own mind and simply didn't notice much of what she did, or mostly even whether she was there or not. Every now and then, her father's tall, gaunt and very stern sister, her aunt Edith, would come to visit for a holiday, and for a while Lucy's meals and schoolwork would be supervised and new clothing would be purchased for her. But Aunt Edith, who was unmarried and childless, was uncomfortable and awkward around children and tended to fuss around her brother. So it was always a relief to all concerned when her holiday ended and things could go back to the way they normally were. Lucy attended the local primary school and did well academically, but she never really made friends with the other children, who reminded her of a twittering flock of silly little birds. Her real education took place after school, as she wandered through the forest, with a book in her hand, identifying plants and taking samples of leaves and flowers to draw and paint.

When Lucy was about twelve years old, a tall, stooped, balding man moved into the cottage next door. From the very beginning Lucy felt that there was something creepy about him and she hid behind her father when the man came round to introduce himself. *"Good evening, sir, I'm Jack Brown, your new neighbour. And who is this pretty little angel?"* he asked, licking his thick, red lips as he stretched out a hand to pinch Lucy's cheek, his small, sunken eyes roving over her skinny, tanned legs that were inadequately covered by her too-small, skimpy sundress.

"Say hello to Mr. Brown, Lucy," her father ordered and, with great reluctance, she shook the soft, clammy hand proffered. Later on Lucy told her father that she didn't like Mr. Brown, but her father said that they should be kind to him because he had lost his forestry job for medical reasons and his wife had left him, taking their only child with her.

Mr. Brown seemed to spend all his time on his wraparound porch, snooping on the neighbourhood. Lucy made a point of walking the long way round to school so that she didn't have to walk past Mr. Brown's house, but somehow he always seemed to be watching her from his porch when she looked up from whatever she was doing in the yard. Lucy decided to time her visits to the forest when Mr. Brown went indoors, so she ended up spending a lot of time watching him too. On the rare occasions that Lucy's father had to leave the house, Mr. Brown would invariably appear at Lucy's front door, on some pretence or another, in an attempt to inveigle his way into their house. Lucy tried to talk to her father about the problem, but he thought that she was imagining it all.

One late summer afternoon Lucy slipped out into the forest when Mr. Brown had briefly disappeared indoors. She was busy trying to identify some mushrooms that had sprung up overnight after a few days of good rain, when suddenly the tranquillity was shattered by a rasping voice, "*Well, just look what I've found – a little forest fairy! What are you doing, my angel?*" Lucy whirled round to find Mr. Brown, standing right next to her, peering over her shoulder.

She backed up against the tree behind her and stuttered, "*Um... Mr. Brown, how did you... um, I didn't hear you,*" Lucy faltered as she watched Mr. Brown lick his lips and step a little closer, grabbing her upper arm in a surprisingly tight grip.

"*What a pretty little thing you are! Give your uncle Jack a kiss, sweetheart,*" he growled, as he pulled her closer. Lucy watched in horror as the thick, wet lips descended towards her face. Her heart pounding, she instinctively kicked out at Mr. Brown's shins, at the same time twisting her arm out of his grasp. "*Little bitch! Didn't your father teach you to* respect your elders?" she heard him spit out as he bent down to rub his shins, watching her sprint away into the forest.

In terror, Lucy ran blindly through the trees, Mr. Brown crashing through the undergrowth after her, cursing at the top of his lungs, "*Dammit brat! Come back here! I'll teach you a lesson or two you'll never forget.*" After a while Lucy reached the rocky outcrop that marked the border between the forest and the deep gorge up ahead. She could no longer hear anyone pursuing her and she sank down onto a rock, quivering with shock and exhaustion. She didn't know what she was going to do. She would have to return home at some point soon, as it was getting late, but she was too afraid that Mr. Brown would be lying in wait for her, now that he had discovered the only path through the dense undergrowth into the forest. She had just decided to chance a stealthy return when, from behind a nearby tree, she heard a soft, wheedling voice, "*Come out, little angel; you can't escape your uncle Jack. Come out and play with me!*" Lucy jumped up and stared wildly around her; there was no escape – she was right up against the rocky overhang, with the deep forested gorge below. As Mr. Brown emerged from behind a tree, he caught sight of her and smiled triumphantly, "*Gotcha! Do you like to play games, my precious? Well, now it's time for some grown-up games! Your uncle Jack was a forester, didn't you realise? I know my way around here and I can move as silently as an owl if I want to.*" Paralysed by terror, Lucy watched Mr. Brown advancing, as a mouse watches a snake.

Then, suddenly, she felt herself being pulled into a soft, gentle pair of arms and a green glow settled over her, as she heard a voice, deep within her heart, "*Everything's going to be fine, little one, just stay still, you're safe.*"

"*What... where's she gone...?*" Mr. Brown spluttered as he waved his arms wildly in the general vicinity in which he had last seen Lucy. He was so close now that she could see the broken veins in his sunken eyes and the enlarged pores on his prominent, bulbous nose. "*Where the hell are you, little bitch! Don't think you will get away; I've got you!*" Mr. Brown went crashing through the undergrowth right past Lucy. Her heart pounding in her ears, she realized that somehow the Lady had made her invisible to Mr. Brown. She looked up questioningly into her friend's eyes, but the Lady put her finger to her lips and winked at Lucy. Mr. Brown was now alternating between violently beating the undergrowth a meter or two away with a stick and examining the rock face, trying to find a possible hidey hole. As he wandered ever closer to the cliff face, Lucy found herself holding her breath and then, suddenly, she glimpsed a rapid, fiery flash beneath Mr. Brown's feet and he tripped, tumbling down into the gorge with a yell of terror. Lucy tore herself out of the Lady's arms and ran to the edge to look, but Mr. Brown had disappeared from view.

"*Is he... what happened?*" Lucy was shivering and panting with shock. The Lady stood behind her and placed a hand on her shoulder, which immediately calmed her down.

"*This was his own choice and his destiny. He won't be troubling you again,*" her voice spoke directly into Lucy's heart. Lucy started to cry and the Lady sank down onto the forest floor, cradling Lucy in her arms, crooning a strange, wild, wordless song that made Lucy think of wind whistling in the trees and birdsong and crickets and frogs and...

When Lucy awoke she was all alone and it was almost dusk. She made her way back home without incident; her fears somehow vanquished. The next day her father told her that Mr. Brown had met with an accident in the forest – he had fallen to his death on the rocks at the bottom of the gorge. Lucy never told a soul about what had really happened that day in the forest until she met Evie, almost sixty years later. But she cherished the secret knowledge of her loving, green friend in her heart and it warmed and comforted her whenever she felt lonely, fearful or sad.

When Lucy was sixteen, she fell in love. His name was Jethro and he wasn't at all like the other irritating, spotty, loud, teenaged boys at her school. He was a loner, just as she was. However, in Jethro's case, his individuality didn't mark him out for mockery or even for being overlooked and ignored; it simply made him cooler. Jethro was tall and slender with dark, curly hair and slate-grey eyes and Lucy's heart lurched and fluttered every time she looked at him. When he happened to walk past her, she would furiously blush, her hands would go all clammy and her mouth would dry out. All the girls in the school vied for Jethro's attention and the boys attempted, with varying degrees of success, to emulate his air of quiet superiority. It was patently obvious to Lucy that Jethro was different and very special and Lucy knew, deep down in her soul, that he was The One for her. But Lucy also knew that she had absolutely no chance of attracting Jethro's attention, as she wasn't, or so she thought, pretty and vivacious. She also knew nothing whatsoever about fashion and make-up and flirting and all the other things that seemed to work for normal girls. She was small and under-developed and quiet and mousy and not at all the kind of girl who would attract the attention of someone as perfect as Jethro.

One afternoon Lucy was packing up her books after her final class of the day. She always took her time over this task as she preferred to leave the classroom last so that it wasn't as obvious that she had no friends and would be walking home alone. As she buckled up her satchel, a shadow fell over her desk and she looked up; right into the gorgeous grey eyes of her dream boy. *"Hi Lucy,"* he said in his quiet, deep voice. *"Can I walk you home today?"* Lucy's heart just about stopped and the blood began singing in her ears. This just couldn't be true – it must be some kind of mistake!

Then, realizing that Jethro was waiting for a response from her, she stammered, in a weak, breathless, little voice, *"Um, are you, um... sure?"* And then she felt a hot tide of embarrassment flooding her face and chest and igniting her ears like glowing embers. *"Um, I mean, um, ok... if you want,"* she quickly clarified, in case he changed his mind.

"Let's go," said Jethro, a man of few words, as he grabbed her satchel and led the way out of the classroom.

For the first few hundred metres, neither of them said a word and Lucy wished that the ground would open up and swallow her because she was convinced that Jethro was already regretting his decision. Also, she had absolutely no idea of how to talk to him and was equally convinced that, even if she could find some miraculous way to open her mouth and find her voice, she anyway had nothing interesting to say. She felt herself getting smaller and smaller until, just before she turned into a little grey mouse and scurried away to hide under a bush, Jethro cleared his throat and said, *"So, how do you like living next to the forest? You must know of some pretty neat places to escape from the world?"*

Lucy, who was finally able to lift her eyes from the ground, gave Jethro a look of pure, unadulterated gratitude and adoration and suddenly found her voice, *"Oh, it's really cool. I have all kinds of special hidey holes and secret places that nobody else knows of."* Then she spent the next few hundred paces mentally kicking herself. Crikey... hidey holes!! He would think that she was just a stupid little kid!

But Jethro smiled and said, *"I'd like to see some of those places. Why don't we go for a walk?"* And then he took hold of her hand and there she was, Lucy-the-grey-mouse, walking hand-in-hand with the coolest kid in the whole school! A tide of pure joy washed over her and it was all she could do not to skip and run down the road like a kid.

When they got to Lucy's house, they dumped their school bags on the porch and then, after a quick glass of juice each, Lucy took Jethro's hand and led him down her special path into the forest. She was feeling very excited and skittish and so, once they were under the canopy, she started running; weaving between the trees, giggling and glancing over her shoulder to make sure that Jethro was following. For the first time ever she felt like a normal girl; silly and playful and flirtatious and she was having the time of her life. Lucy was much smaller and faster than Jethro and so, after a while, she slowed down a bit to allow him to catch up with her. Jethro grabbed her from behind and she squealed with excitement as he lifted her up in the air and spun her around, tickling her as he set her down. Lucy giggled and squirmed and playfully pushed Jethro away and then leaned back against a tree trunk, relishing beneath her fingertips the velvety softness of the moss covering its bark. Never had she felt so alive, so vital and so happy. She was In Love and everything was absolutely perfect. And then her cup of joy completely overflowed when Jethro leaned in and kissed her gently on her cheek. She reached up a trembling hand and tentatively touched the side of his cheek and then let her fingertips explore his eyebrows, his forehead and then, daringly, outline his beautiful lips. Jethro put his hands on Lucy's shoulders and pulled her up against him and then he started kissing her lips, hard and searchingly and Lucy found herself responding. This was what she had always dreamed of! This was her wildest fantasies, all come true at once!

But then Lucy felt Jethro's hands begin to roam all over her body and suddenly she felt out of breath and out of control. Everything was just moving too fast for her and she had no idea of how to make it stop. Or even whether she wanted it to stop. Lucy could feel the entire length of Jethro's body pressing her against the tree and his tongue was in her mouth and then she felt his fingers beginning to explore her breast and she started to panic. She tried to move her head away and pull his hands away from her body, but Jethro was far too occupied to even notice her feeble attempts.

Just as Lucy was gearing up to push Jethro away and destroy forever her chances with him, she opened her eyes and noticed that the Lady was standing right behind Jethro. Lucy gasped and Jethro must have felt something change, as he lifted his head and said in a husky voice, *"What... what's going on?"* Noticing that Lucy was looking behind him, he asked, *"What are you looking at?"* and turned around, to find himself staring right into the emerald-green eyes of the Lady. Lucy never did find out what it was that Jethro thought he saw that day, but he yelled at the top of his lungs, his voice breaking somewhat at the end; staggered back and then took off like a bat out of hell, his air of cool superiority discarded as he ran for his life through the trees, never once stopping to look behind him again.

"What... What did you do that for? You've scared him!" Lucy yelled at the Lady. *"Jethro, it's OK, come back!"* she called, but Jethro was long gone. *"How could you! You've spoiled everything. He's never going to want to be with me,*

ever again! I hate you! You've ruined my life! Just leave me alone!" Lucy screamed at the Lady with increasing volume, but the Deva simply smiled, turned around and glided away into the trees. *"Dammit!"* Lucy cursed, grabbing a stick and beating away at the undergrowth in frustration. After she had exhausted herself, she turned around and stomped back home, kicking at stones in the path as she went. But, in some secret part of herself, Lucy was just a little bit relieved that the Lady had saved her the embarrassment of telling Jethro to stop. She knew that she hadn't been ready for what he had had in mind. In an even deeper secret part of herself she felt really disappointed that her idol had behaved just like a scared little girl, running away without even checking to see if she, Lucy, was ok.

That Jethro wasn't the right guy for her after all was made abundantly clear when she overheard him bragging to another boy at school the next day that he had won the bet they had made about whether he could get "mousy little Lucy" past first base. Lucy felt utterly humiliated and she responded by withdrawing even further into herself and into her solitary nature studies in the forest. Boys were simply a stupid waste of time anyway, she told herself. By and by she forgave the Lady because she realized that she had actually been saved from making an even bigger fool of herself by her green friend. But, although she often spoke aloud to the Lady as she worked in the forest, she was not to see her again for a very, very long time.

Lucy's years of self-study in the forest stood her in good stead when she was offered a full scholarship to study Botany at university when she finished school. On the day that Lucy left for university, she walked into the forest to visit all of her favourite places for the last time. She had hoped that the Lady might appear to say goodbye, but, despite calling her, no-one appeared, and it was with a very heavy heart that Lucy bid her beloved forest goodbye. She was not to return for several years.

After graduating, Lucy made a name for herself, firstly as a passionate, gifted researcher and lecturer, and then later as a professor of Botany. She published several self-illustrated books and scientific papers on the unique floral kingdom in which she had spent her formative years. She travelled all over the world and presented talks about her research and she lectured on Botany to successive years of university students. In time, she married a colleague who shared her interests and they bought a beautiful home in the city, close to the university where they both worked. Lucy's life was happy and fulfilled and, for the first time, the aching loneliness that had always been her constant companion, abated somewhat and she started to come out of her shell and to make friends. For the next few years, Lucy hardly ever went back home to her father's cottage, as there was always so much to do. Even when her father passed away and she inherited the cottage, Lucy was still unable to ever find more than a few days a year to spend in her childhood home.

In her late thirties, Lucy and her husband decided that it was time to start a family and, eventually, after several months of trying, Lucy finally fell pregnant. She was elated. This was the cherry on top of the cake! She walked around with a permanent grin on her face and found herself humming as she went about her daily work. She scaled back her teaching and travelling and joyfully prepared for the new addition to her family.

Very early on a cold, grey winter's morning in her third month of pregnancy, Lucy awoke with a start, her heart thumping wildly in her chest. An icy sense of dread gripped her throat and she knew that something was very, very wrong. An hour or two later, in a chaos of tears, sweat, blood and excruciating pain, Lucy's baby slipped away from her without ever having had a chance to live.

When Lucy's doctor told her that the chances of her ever falling pregnant again were very slim and that the baby would never have been carried to term anyway, it felt as though a heavy, iron portcullis came clanging down around her heart. Lucy spent the next three months in a dreary miasma of despair, interspersed with guilt; only briefly emerging to rage against the world, before sinking even deeper into apathy and isolation. Her husband was loving and supportive, but as the months stretched on and Lucy sank ever deeper and deeper into depression and self-loathing, his patience eventually wore thin. Despite counselling, anti-depressants, holidays, changes of diet, vitamins and every other possible remedy, Lucy simply couldn't pull herself back into the world of the living again. After a year, her husband gave Lucy an ultimatum, *"Pull yourself together or I'm leaving,"* he told her. Lucy did try, very hard, to improve. But, in the end, it merely felt as if she were trying to paste a tiny band-aid onto a gaping, mortal wound in her soul and she hurtled right back down into the deepest pits of despair. After another three months, her husband left her and six months later they were officially divorced. In a way, it was a relief for Lucy to no longer have to pretend to be recovering. She took a leave of absence from work and went to stay in the little cottage at the edge of the forest.

For two weeks Lucy remained in bed, sleeping all day with the covers pulled over her head; lying awake all night, wresting with her inner demons. She hardly ate and found that showering or changing her clothing was simply too much effort, so she didn't bother. At the end of the second week, Lucy's Aunt Edith arrived and, without ceremony, marched into Lucy's room, pulled off her bedclothes and dumped a bucket of cold water over her head. Gasping and spluttering with shock, Lucy jumped out of bed and glared at her Aunt. *"Good, you're up. Now, give me those smelly pyjamas and go get into the shower,"* she commanded. Lucy was so angry that she couldn't even find her voice to retaliate and so she did as she was told. An hour later, after a shower, a change of clothing and a breakfast of cooked oats and fruit, Edith banished Lucy from the house and told her to go for a walk. It was just too much effort to resist Edith's dictates and so Lucy found her feet carrying her down the familiar path through the garden gate and into the forest.

Without even noticing where she was going, within half an hour Lucy found herself standing in front of the giant Yellowwood tree she remembered so well from her childhood – the tree amongst whose roots she had so often sheltered from the scary outside world. Lucy noticed that the light was different from what she had remembered and then she realized that there was a large gap in the leaf canopy overhead, which had previously been filled by the spreading branches of a gnarled old Ironwood tree. The dead and rotting tree trunk was lying on the ground, covered in moss and fungi. As Lucy gazed at the space that the tree had previously occupied, she felt again the gnawing, aching emptiness in her womb and once again the dreary, familiar tears started to course down her cheeks. She closed her eyes and wished that she could simply leave her life; wished that she didn't have to go on, for she felt that there was nothing worth living for any more.

Then Lucy sensed a stillness and felt a warm glow on her face and arms. She opened her eyes to find the Lady standing before her. It had been a very long time since Lucy had last seen the Lady, but she still looked exactly the same; still beautiful, still young. The Lady looked at Lucy with infinite kindness and love in her eyes. She stretched out her hand and placed it on Lucy's belly and a gentle, warm, healing glow began to pulse through Lucy's body. Then the Lady slowly lifted her hand away and Lucy gasped as she felt the emptiness, the ache within, being pulled from her, and being replaced by a feeling of warmth and completion. The Lady turned her hand upwards and lifted it until it was level with Lucy's eyes and Lucy could see that there was a tiny seed in the palm of her companion's hand. The Lady took the seed between her fingers and, bending down; she buried it in the forest floor, beneath the opening in the canopy left by the fallen Ironwood tree. Then she stood up again and touched the palm of her hand to Lucy's heart and suddenly the iron portcullis that had been protecting Lucy's broken heart burst open and, with it, the emotional floodgates opened. Lucy fell to her hands and knees. She dropped her head and began to howl; deep, primal, gut-wrenching, animal sobs that wracked her entire body. And she cried for her lost baby and for all the babies she would never have; she cried for her broken marriage and for her career; she cried for her lonely childhood and she cried most of all for the loss of her mother when she was only a little girl. And her tears soaked into the ground where the little seed had been planted by the Lady.

When Lucy was finally emptied of every last tear, she realized that she felt a lot lighter; something had changed... she had changed. She sat back on her haunches and looked up, with red, swollen eyes, into the endlessly kind and compassionate emerald-green eyes of the Lady. And, for the first time in eighteen months, she smiled; a quivering, watery little smile, to be sure, but a smile, nonetheless. The Lady smiled back at Lucy and then pointed to the ground in front of her. Lucy looked down and, to her amazement, she saw that a tiny little seedling had started to sprout from the seed that the Lady had planted and which Lucy had watered with her grief. As Lucy watched in wonderment, the seedling rapidly grew before her very eyes, twisting and turning as it sprouted branches and tender, pale green leaves, which quickly darkened and proliferated. Within minutes the tree was as tall as Lucy was. She scrambled to her feet and watched the tree grow until it was at least five metres tall, at which point beautiful, white flowers began to bloom until the tree resembled a bride in all her lacy finery. Lucy gasped at the beauty before her. Although she was an expert in the plants of this region, she had never before encountered a tree such as this. Then the flowers began to turn brown and fall off the tree and then seedpods started to appear and lengthen where the flowers had previously been. Within minutes the tree was covered in long, narrow, green pods, which started to brown and then... with a series of barely audible little clicks, the dried seedpods began to open.

To Lucy's utter amazement, out of each seedpod emerged flutters of tiny white butterflies, which alit upon her outstretched arms and hands, her head, her nose, her ears, her shoulders, until she was absolutely covered in tiny, tickling insects. Lucy laughed in delight at the sheer wonder of it all and then the butterflies left her, like a great, soft, white, living cloak, which flapped a few times around the tree before departing into the forest like a puffy white, living cloud.

Lucy watched the butterflies go with a sense of joy and gratitude and, as she looked back at her companion, she heard the Lady speaking within her heart, *"Human beings are capable of magnificent acts of creation and nurturing. One of the most beautiful and mystical of these is the bearing and the raising of a child. However, for you, it was not meant to be that you should expend your creativity and energies in the raising of a child, but rather in the finding and giving of your own unique gift to the world."* As Lucy's eyes misted over with tears, she felt the truth of what the Lady had said resonating within her deepest being. She sat down beneath the magical tree and spent the rest of the afternoon just being still in the silence of the place. When she got back to the cottage that evening, she fell into bed without even removing her clothing and she slept a deep, dreamless, healing sleep for the first time in over a year.

The next morning Lucy awoke just after dawn, refreshed and feeling hopeful and energetic in a way that was completely foreign to her. She climbed out of bed, wrapped an old woollen shawl around herself and pulled on her hiking boots without socks. Then she grabbed her long-abandoned easel out of the hall closet, set it up in a shady spot in the garden and began to paint.

Lucy never returned to the university. She stayed on in her father's cottage, barely even noticing the passage of time as she was swept along on a wave of abundant creativity. She drew and painted and wrote, first poems, then illustrated short stories for children, then novellas for adults and finally, novels, all set in the enchanting, forested world with which she was so familiar. Her great outpouring of creativity began to provide a comfortable living for her and she was able to continue staying in the cottage at the edge of the forest, supporting herself with her creative outputs. She became rather eccentric in her heedless pursuit of her muse and local folklore soon abounded with tales of the strange lady who would roam the forest in her nightgown and hiking boots, drawing and writing and talking to herself, as she developed plotlines and stories in her mind.

And so the years passed. Lucy no longer felt lonely or alone, even though she very rarely spent time with any human company outside of the characters in her stories. The only exception to this was her little neighbour, Evie, with whom Lucy felt some special connection and with whom she shared her precious memories of her encounters with the Lady. Lucy was self-contained and fulfilled and content and that was enough for her.

One morning Lucy awoke just as the first rosy fingers of dawn were gently caressing the hilltops on the horizon. It felt like an important day, but she couldn't for the life of her think why that should be so. She had, just the previous evening, finally finished a commission of five paintings for a client, with which she was extremely pleased. Finally, her knowledge of Botany, her artistic skills and technique and her love of story had come together in the production of five beautiful, magical pieces of art, which were the finest she had ever produced. For the first time in over twenty years, she had no unfinished creative work to attend to. She stretched out her aching back and then massaged her stiff fingers as she relished the unaccustomed freedom of the day ahead with nothing that she had to do and nowhere that she had to be.

Suddenly she heard a beautiful, crystal-clear chirping sound and, glancing out of her window, she glimpsed an iridescent little blue bird on her windowsill. The little bird puffed out its chest, shook its feathers and then flew away with a jubilant, high-pitched, musical chirping, leaving Lucy feeling inexplicably elated.

After breakfast Lucy still had no idea of what she would do and could still not recall why that day of all days should feel so significant, so she decided to go for a walk in the forest to clear her mind. Within minutes her feet were treading the familiar path that she had taken a thousand times before: through the garden gate, down the bramble-covered path and into the forest. Lucy walked a lot slower nowadays and she needed a stick to maintain her balance on the uneven path, so it took her almost an hour to reach her special place beneath the massive old Yellowwood tree. When she got there, she was feeling very out of breath, so she leaned up against the tree, her hands tightly clasped to her chest, gasping for breath. But, despite resting there for a good while, Lucy's heart kept racing and suddenly she began to feel very dizzy and waves of nausea began rolling across her chest. She swallowed hard and bent down over her knees, clutching the tree for balance. Then Lucy became aware of shooting pains in her back and neck and her jaw felt strangely tight. She started to panic as she realized that nobody on Earth knew where she was and that there was no way she could walk back to her cottage in order to phone for assistance.

Lucy was just beginning to feel faint with pain and fear when she glanced up and noticed a familiar pale green glow moving towards her. It was the Lady and Lucy had never felt so relieved to see anyone in her entire life. The Lady calmly glided up to Lucy and, with a gentle, compassionate smile, placed both her hands on Lucy's chest. Instantly the dizziness and nausea lifted and the pain receded, allowing Lucy to stand up straight and look her dear old friend in the eyes. "*Thank you,*" she whispered, noticing that the Lady still looked as young and beautiful as she had the very first time that Lucy had met her, at age four.

The Lady, continuing to gaze into Lucy's eyes, brought forth, with infinite tenderness, an egg from Lucy's heart. As Lucy looked in wonderment at the egg in her friend's hand, it began to crack open and a tiny little blue bird emerged, shaking and fluffing its feathers. With a great sense of joy, Lucy recognized the little bird she had seen on her windowsill earlier that morning. The bird lifted its beak and the most exquisitely pure notes emerged from its throat. Lucy watched, enthralled, until the song finished, and then the little bird fluffed out its feathers once more, looked her in the eye, blinked once or twice and flew off into the forest.

The Lady took Lucy's hands in both of hers and spoke, deep into her heart, words of wisdom and compassion, "*Your heartsong is over now, my friend,*" and Lucy knew that it was true and a sense of deep peace, quiet joy, relief and serenity washed over her. And then the Lady and Lucy walked hand-in-hand, following the little blue bird into the forest.

Author's note: I wrote Lucy's story as a birthday gift for my dear friend, Ashleigh, who has given me permission to reprint the story in this book. This was the story that provided the inspiration and the starting point for my book, The Green Lady.

CHAPTER 3
EXPRESSION OF THE
AUTHENTIC SELF

"*My next slide is a photograph of Acacia mearnsii, the Australian black wattle. This tree was originally brought into South Africa in 1864 for shade, fuel, windbreaks and later to provide tannins for use in the leather tanning industry. The black wattle is one of the most widespread invasive alien trees in South Africa. It outcompetes indigenous plants for nitrogen, water and organic materials and significantly reduces catchment water. Black wattle is estimated to have invaded over 2.5 million hectares in South Africa. The species forms very dense stands of evergreen trees and frequently replaces seasonally dormant grasslands and fynbos.*"

I was listening to an extremely informative talk on the indigenous and invader plants species of the Garden Route region, presented by retired botanist, Dr Benjamin Leigh. As the weeks passed and I accumulated more and more stories about appearances of the Green Lady and other supernatural happenings in the Knysna forest, I began to feel that I should educate myself about the plants of the area. Hence my attendance of this presentation. Dr Leigh had worked for over forty years in the South African Department of Water Affairs and Forestry and was recognized as a leading expert on South Africa's forests and fynbos biome. He had retired to Knysna five years earlier, but continued to share his extensive knowledge by presenting a monthly talk on some aspect of the region's indigenous plant species at a local community centre. Tonight's presentation focused on the management of invasive alien vegetation, apparently one of Dr Leigh's abiding passions.

After the talk, I helped myself to a cup of tea and approached Dr Leigh, who was surrounded by a group of people demanding his attention. When an opportunity finally arose to ask my question, I feared that Dr Leigh, as a man of science, would dismiss it out of hand. But I decided to ask it anyway, as my experiences in gathering the material required for my book had begun to inure me to the potential shame of being considered a flake!

"Dr Leigh, my name is Peter Allen. I'm a journalist and I'm writing a book on the many encounters with supernatural beings in the forests of this area. Have you ever personally encountered any such beings, specifically a Green Lady, during your work in the forest?" I took a deep breath and braced myself, fully expecting Dr Leigh to either disregard both my question and myself, or else to ridicule me for my gullibility. He remained silent for a few seconds, frowning as he regarded me with an intense blue stare from beneath bushy, grey eyebrows.

Then, apparently having reached a decision, he handed me a business card, saying as he did so, *"Give me a call tomorrow and we'll set up a time to meet,"* and then he turned to answer a question about invasive alien management strategies from the woman to his right.

Two days later I met up with Dr Leigh, who insisted that I call him Ben, and his gentle and softly-spoken wife, Belinda, at their home on a two-hectare smallholding with magnificent views over hectares of fynbos, with indigenous-forested gorges and the Outeniqua Mountains in the distance. Ben told me that Belinda's retirement occupations included needlework and watercolour painting, but that he became restless if he sat around too much. So, he spent his time on his greatest passion, namely, invasive alien vegetation management. Ben was engaged in his own personal titanic battle with the black wattle, in which each tree he removed was counted as a personal victory. He was very aware that black wattle eradication in South Africa would never be achieved, or at least not during his lifetime. But he could (and did) keep his own land clear, as well as the surrounding areas that could be viewed from the large porch at the front of his wooden home, which was built on poles in order to maximally benefit from the view. Indeed, as I stood on Ben's porch, looking out at the view of mountains, fynbos and indigenous forest, there were very few black wattles to be seen, and those only on his neighbours' properties. Ben's bête noir was the fact that there was very little he could do to compel his neighbours to clear their own land of invasive aliens. *"And they're contaminating the water courses with wattle seeds, which get carried downstream to re-infest previously-cleared land!"* he fumed. This was definitely a very passionate man on a mission!

'*So, you wanted to talk about the Lady,"* Ben said, once he had collected himself and we were seated inside, enjoying a cup of coffee and some home-made cookies.

"Have you seen her?" I asked, elated that Ben was willing to so directly approach the topic. I had expected to have to gradually sidle up to the subject so as not to alienate my host.

"I have indeed, young man. In fact, I would go so far as to say that she's the reason that I'm still alive today!" Intrigued, I leaned in so as not to miss a single word of Ben's story...

Ben had purchased his smallholding, which had been absolutely choked with wattle and other alien species, using a portion of his pension payout. Whilst their home was being built, he began his work of clearing invasive alien vegetation off his land. Ben informed me that one does not clear black wattle only once. *"The buggers drop kilograms of seed and so, even when you have chopped down the original large trees, properly applying stump treatment to prevent re-growth and coppicing and pulled up the saplings and seedlings, you are left with a massive seed bank, which continues to germinate over the next few years. So, each portion of cleared land must be revisited, year after year, to hand pull thousands-upon-thousands of seedlings. Fortunately, as the indigenous vegetation returns, it begins to exert its own control over the black wattle and, eventually, after revisiting a parcel of land three or four times, there are virtually no wattles left. This is really a labour of love and absolutely back-breaking work, but what a pleasure it is to see the diversity of indigenous grasses, flowers, bushes and, eventually, trees, returning to what once was practically a monoculture of black wattle. Of course, there are plenty of other alien species as well: Australian Black Wood, Rooikrans, Port Jackson, Hakea, Eucalypts, Bugweed... oh, so many, many more!"* As Ben spoke, I could clearly witness his passion and love for the land and it made me feel as if the world was a slightly better and kinder place because he was out there every day, gifting his time and energy to the forest.

Ben not only cleared his own land, but also the government-owned land between his smallholding and the start of the indigenous forest. As Ben put it, *"Belinda and I were the ones most affected by the alien vegetation on the land adjoining mine and, having worked in government for all those years, I was very aware of the budgetary, time and manpower constraints. I guess I just wanted to do my bit and continue to feel useful whilst on pension. Of course, it helps to keep me in shape, not to mention, out of Belinda's hair!"*

One warm, early spring morning, Ben was once more hard at work with his trusty bowsaw, cutting down adolescent wattles on a piece of land about a kilometre from his home. As he pushed through dense, shoulder-high fynbos, he heard a sound which provoked blood curdling terror in the most ancient part of his brain. It was a loud, continuous, hissing sound, which Ben knew meant one thing only – puffadder! The puffadder is a highly venomous, extremely aggressive snake, responsible for most snakebite fatalities in Africa. Ben stopped dead in his tracks and anxiously looked around, his heart pounding in his ears. There it was! Less than a meter ahead of him was the furiously puffing snake, its thick, heavy, brown-banded body tightly coiled on the ground, ready to strike. Ben was aware that the puffadder will strike suddenly, at high speed and with great force. He also knew that just one hundred milligrams of cytotoxic puffadder venom can kill an adult human male within a day. He remained frozen to the spot, keeping the furious, hissing snake in his view and hoping for a miracle.

Just then, Ben heard a rustling sound to his left and, keeping one eye on the snake, he quickly glanced up, only to have his poor thumping heart dealt yet another shock. A beautiful, naked Green Lady wrapped in her own dark-green hair, was standing, just a couple of metres away to his left. Ben wondered whether he was experiencing a stress-induced hallucination or even whether he was having a stroke, but then the Lady held up her hand, palm forward towards Ben, clearly indicating that he should remain where he was, and she turned towards the snake. She made a few puffing exhalations through her open mouth and the snake immediately lowered its head, uncoiled and silently vanished through the undergrowth.

Still not moving his body, Ben turned his head towards the Lady, wondering as he did so whether the threat of the snake had been replaced by an even greater threat. *"Th.. tha... thank you!"* he stammered and her answering smile reassured him that she represented no immediate danger to him. Then Ben became aware of words spoken by the Lady, directly into his mind, as she gazed intently at him with her shining, emerald-green eyes.

"Ben, you are a friend of the forest. You give of your own time and energy in an attempt to bring about greater balance, harmony and health. You redress some of the evils committed by others of your species and so you will never be harmed in this place. You are under my own personal protection."

Ben answered simply and honestly, *"I love this place; it feeds my soul."*

A warm, gentle smile illuminating her face, the Lady responded, *"And that love, my dear friend, and your positive intentions, though you may not understand at present, are a far greater gift to the forest than thousands of hours spent doing battle with the black wattle."*

"But, I don't understand! Does that mean that I should stop trying to manage invasive, alien vegetation then?" asked Ben, feeling somewhat bewildered.

"No, by all means, continue doing the excellent work that you do. It is an expression of your most authentic self and also the way in which you evolve your consciousness. It's all about perspective, you see. A human being has a perspective of a few, short years only. Even those humans with the greatest vision think, at most, only a couple of hundred years ahead. But, for the forest, the perspective is one of hundreds of thousands, even millions, of years. And, from that perspective, invasive species come and go. Natural predators of invaders will arise and become extinct. In fact, humans are merely one of many species that will eventually, and perhaps sooner than they anticipate, become extinct, and again the forest will re-grow and come to dominate the planet, only to die back again as the climate changes and then re-grow a few hundred thousand years later. Cycles within cycles of life. So, you see, your efforts change the world only for a very short time and only for yourself and perhaps a few others. But your loving intent... well, this changes absolutely everything! Love evolves the consciousness of the All."

Ben was still trying to absorb what the Lady had told him when she winked at him, smiled again and faded away before his very eyes. He was left feeling completely bewildered and rather shaken up and unsure of himself. The experience would, over the following months, cause Ben to question much of what he had previously taken for granted. But, after intense contemplation, Ben gradually started to understand the message the forest had given him.

"You see, Peter," he said, his fierce intellect shining through his warm, wise blue gaze, "It's about finding balance *and harmony within ourselves. We accomplish this by continually seeking, honouring and expressing our most authentic selves, which is, by the way, the highest purpose we can hope to strive for in this world. In my case, currently the most authentic expression of myself is the active management of alien vegetation, but in your case it might be the growing of vegetables, the painting of a picture, the running of a business, or even, possibly, the writing of a book,"* he winked at me. *"Our most authentic expression of self also changes over the years as we become more-and-more of who we truly are and less-and-less of what others want and expect us to be. By expressing our most authentic selves, we restore harmony and balance within ourselves, which creates the closest experience of heaven on Earth that we can have in this limited human form. Of course, our authentic expressions are also the greatest expression of Love that we have to offer to the world. So, for me, right now, chopping down wattles becomes the most loving gift I can bring to myself and therefore to the great unity of which we are all a part."*

I left Ben's home imbued with a profound sense of peace and joy. It appeared that even my second-hand encounters with the Lady were leaving an indelible impression upon me. I only wished that I might meet this mysterious Lady of the forest for myself.

CHAPTER 4
LISTEN TO YOUR HEART

I met Sandi and Greg at the house warming party of Jenny, whom I had met in the Knysna library, where I was researching the history of the town and she was returning her library books. In the group of casually clad farmers and eclectically clad hippies, Sandi and Greg stood out like two sore thumbs! Their clothing was stylish and clearly expensive, albeit no longer new, and they exuded an unmistakable whiff of sophistication that spoke to me of city dwellers. My journalistic instincts informed me that here was potentially a story worth investigating, and was I ever glad that I followed those instincts! This, then, is the story of Sandi and Greg.

Sandi and Greg were in their early forties when they moved to Knysna from Johannesburg. Sandi had been working long, stressful hours as a corporate management consultant and Greg was a partner in a top IT consulting company. They had plenty of disposable income, expensive tastes, no children and, as they put it, a "work hard, play even harder" approach to life. They owned a designer yuppie pad in a very desirable part of the city, drove sports cars, wore fashionable, quality clothing, travelled extensively, both for work and leisure and generally lived the lifestyle that most people aspire to. But, somehow, something was missing.

As Sandi put it, "*I looked at the people who were above me in the corporate food chain - those jobs to which I was supposed to aspire and toward which I was supposed to be working - and I thought, "Is that it? Is that all I can look forward to? Years-and-years of insane working hours and personal sacrifice to achieve THAT!" Yes, they had tons of cash and all of the toys and ego gratifications that money could buy, but none of them appeared to be happy. They all had dysfunctional relationships, unhappy children and poor health. They were sick and stressed-out and miserable. I knew that I wanted something different for myself. Besides, I had had enough of a taste of the so-called "high-life" to realize that it didn't really satisfy me. The fancy stuff just doesn't fill the gap inside. I wanted much more than that.*"

Greg agreed, "*It's all a trap. Shiny, new stuff is only exciting for a minute before you need the next fix. Increases and bonuses are rapidly absorbed into your lifestyle and you find yourself always adding more-and-more debt. Simply everyone lives above their means so as to have even more stuff to try and make themselves feel better and to keep up with ever-increasing life-style expectations. But, it doesn't work, of course.*"

So, Sandi and Greg decided to quit the rat race, climb off the hamster wheel and try a new way of living. This would be a completely new challenge for them. They resigned their jobs, liquidated their assets and moved to Knysna where they purchased an eight-hectare smallholding in a quiet, remote settlement. They had a big, bold idea that they were going to implement on their land. The idea was to become self-sustaining within five years. Greg had read "*The Self-Sufficient Life and How to Live it*" by John Seymour and he was looking forward to implementing the ideas in the book. The piece of land they purchased was perfect for the objective, as it had no power supply, and therefore electricity would have to be provided by a solar-electrical system. Greg and Sandi would have to collect rainwater and also clean their own wastewater, as there were absolutely no services or amenities provided on their remote piece of land. It was the perfect challenge for two over-achieving, type-A personalities, neither of whom had ever failed at anything they had set their minds and their considerable talents and energies to.

They purchased a caravan in which they would stay whilst they built their own home themselves. The home would be made of sandbags and they would lay out their fully organic vegetable garden according to permaculture principles. They told their friends and family that they would be like modern frontiers-people, boldly implementing a mix of ancient and very modern technologies to live a completely self-sustainable lifestyle, which would be a glowing example to all of how it should be done.

"Oh, I'm actually SO embarrassed to recall how very naive we were!" Sandi laughed, shaking her head.

"Did things not turn out the way you had planned?" I enquired.

"And then some!" she giggled. "I can laugh about it now, but back then the series of disasters that followed nearly broke us, physically, emotionally and financially!"

The first thing they did was to build a storage dam for irrigation water. But, in Sandi's words, "We failed to properly observe, or take into account, the conditions on our land during the planning of the dam and so we ended up digging the dam in exactly the wrong place. When the abundant Knysna rains arrived to fill up our dam, we realized that the dam's overflow was perfectly positioned to flood our home *every time there was a heavy rainfall! So, back to the drawing board then on that one!"*

The next disaster was in the building of their home. The idea was to use materials that were abundant right there on the farm and so the soil that was removed to build the dam would go into the sandbags to build their home. Unfortunately, the soil on their smallholding was thick, heavy clay and not at all suitable for sandbag building. They also underestimated the magnitude of the job of filling the bags and stacking them to build their home. It was backbreaking, unrelenting work and apparently required a certain level of skill that they just didn't possess, despite all the books they had read, as their first attempt caved in, just a couple of weeks after building was finally completed. For their second attempt, they were able to access telephonic input from someone who had built using this method before, and the result therefore remained standing. However, the clay they had used to fill the bags absorbed water during an intensely rainy season and the bags began to split. Sandi and Greg realized that the method was called "sandbag building" for a reason. The bags needed to be filled with sand and not with clay! In addition, the clay they had used to clad the outside walls of their home cracked and fell off, thereby exposing the waterproofing membranes and layers beneath, which soon degraded in the extreme weather. After months of effort and ever-mounting costs, they were still living in their caravan.

"The veggie garden was yet another disaster," Greg admitted, with a grimace. They followed permaculture principles and prepared raised beds, using the double-digging system. This was another massive, physically challenging job and Greg freely admits that they were hopelessly overambitious about the size of the garden they had planned.

But, eventually, after much blood, sweat and tears, their garden was ready and they optimistically planted their first heirloom seeds. Within a very short while they realized that the clay soil was extremely unfavourable for the planting of most vegetables, with root crops appearing to be out of the question altogether. The soil required a huge amount of compost and they would have to dig in (literally) tons of sand to lighten the soil mix before they would be able to grow pretty much most crops. This was yet another huge expense and an even bigger job.

Then, once their crops got going, they soon realized that there was going to be plenty of competition for their succulent produce. If it wasn't the neighbour's horses, then it was porcupines, bushbuck, monkeys, baboons or bushpig raiding their garden. It was a delicious all-you-can-eat buffet for the local wildlife! And, in addition, there were rodents and birds and a whole multitude of different insects, snails and even fungi, all of which wanted their share of the bounty. Our intrepid, would-be frontiers-people discovered that organic gardening, although wonderful in theory, is extremely challenging in practice.

Greg and Sandi eventually erected an electric fence around their garden, which proved to be too much for their solar-electric system to handle throughout the night and so they had to upgrade that system, at yet additional expense. However, once the fruit trees and berry bushes starting bearing fruit, they discovered that the baboons were willing to risk a large amount of discomfort in order to access the delicious treats. The baboons were scaling the electric fencing, shrieking all the way as they were shocked, but finding that it was all worth it once they were inside the garden and enjoying their sweet treats. Sandi and Greg had to put up a roofed cage made of gum poles and bird wire around their vegetable garden. Yet another unplanned expense.

Greg and Sandi had decided to clear their wattle-infested land and return it to pristine condition, but no-one had told them that the backbreaking work of clearing needs to be repeated over-and-over-and-over again. Every time they cut down a big wattle tree, millions of tiny wattle seedlings would germinate all around it, causing the couple's courage to sink into their mud-bespattered boots. And, just as one part of their farm was cleared, they would realize that the adjacent portion was due for re-clearing.

"There were just SO many other challenges as well," Sandi recalled. They had erected a plastic sheet between poles in order to collect rainwater to be used for drinking and washing, but they rapidly realized that it didn't provide nearly enough water for even their basic needs. They had to build an open-sided shed with guttering and pipes leading into tanks in order to collect enough rainwater. And then, their solar geyser just didn't heat the water to more than lukewarm and so, even after a long day spent knee deep in thick clay mud, they would only be able to have, at best, a very short, very lukewarm shower.

Their SUV, which had seemed like such a good idea back in the city, kept getting stuck in the thick mud of their driveway. *"In fact, it felt as if we were chronically up to our eyeballs in mud,"* laughed Sandi. *"I would probably have given my right arm for a long soak in a hot, fragrant bath at that point!"* she joked.

"And those bloody baboons..." Greg reminded her. It seemed as if every time they left their land, they would return to find some damage. *"I started to believe that they had a personal vendetta against us!"* exclaimed Greg. The baboons

killed their baby chicks and stole their eggs, uprooted their young trees, ripped off guttering and even broke into their caravan and trashed it. *"The buggers even pushed the microwave oven off the counter, broke all of our crockery, stole our food and ripped open pillows to scatter feathers all over the place,"* recalls Greg.

"And, don't forget Greg, my remaining baby chicks, after the baboons had done their worst, were taken by the forest buzzards. For me, that was the final straw," Sandi admitted, deep sadness still evident on her face, despite these events having occurred years earlier.

At the end of the first eighteen months Sandi finally fell apart. *"We had no home built, no properly productive veggie garden, no operational dam, no decent amenities and we were living in a mud bath. Our land was a money sink and I was physically and emotionally drained. I had completely reached the end of my tether,"* she recalled. *"During a bout of hysterical sobbing, I told Greg that I was going back to the city, with or without him!"*

Greg smiled wryly, *"I was nearly in tears myself! But I finally convinced Sandi to give it one more month and we would find a way to turn it all around. In my heart, though, I had absolutely no idea of how we were going to do that and I knew that I was simply postponing the inevitable,"* he admitted.

That night, just before he fell asleep, Greg was suddenly struck by the realization that he had never, even once, asked even a single person for help on this project. He had just assumed that he and Sandi would easily accomplish this goal, just as they had accomplished everything else in their lives up to that point. *"I wasn't used to asking anyone for help,"* admitted Greg, *"But that night I did. I sent a plea for* help out into the universe to anyone who might be listening. I said, "I really don't know what I'm doing here. If this is right for us to do, please could I have some help and guidance?" and then I guess I fell asleep."

That night Greg had a dream that was to change everything for the couple. "I dreamt that I was standing knee-deep in mud in our veggie garden, looking at the shrivelled leaves of my cabbages that had been decimated by aphids. I was feeling absolutely despondent and at the end of my tether, when I caught a green flash out of the corner of my eye. Looking up, I was astounded to see a very tall, slender, beautiful, naked green woman standing next to me. At first I thought that someone was playing a joke on me, but when I leapt to my feet, I could see that she was very real and that she was smiling gently at me. "Who are you?" I asked, my heart pounding with fear. "I'm the Deva of the forest," she answered, "And I've come to provide you with the assistance for which you have asked." I realized that her lips didn't move when she spoke and that I wasn't hearing her words with my ears, but rather through my heart. Then she said, "This is always going to feel like pushing water uphill and you will never accomplish what you want to accomplish until you first start with the question, "What is my heart telling me to do?" At the moment you are pitting the desires of your ego and the ideas of your mind against the rhythms and harmony of Nature. You have had ample evidence to prove to you that you will never, ever prevail. Discover what your heart is telling you to do, and then do that, always seeking to find your harmony with all that is around you. Stop resisting using your will and your ego. Acceptance is key. Accept, first yourself, then all that is around you. Then you will find yourself in the flow of life and everything will become easy and joyful."

"I had so many objections and questions and fears," recalls Greg, "But when I looked into her emerald-green eyes, I knew, without a shadow of a doubt, that she spoke the truth and that this was the only path open to me now. And then she disappeared and I woke up. I rolled over in bed and shook Sandi awake. Before I could say a word, Sandi said to me, "Greg, we've got it all wrong! We've been trying to do it all ourselves, and we need to ask for help. We need to invite others to co-create this dream with us. We need to share our toys!" Apparently Sandi too had had a visit from the Green Lady!

Sandi and Greg completely changed their plans for their piece of land after that. They approached like-minded friends in the city who also desired to find a new way of living and these friends eventually helped them to create an intentional community of five families. Different people brought different skills to the party and the work, which had been overwhelming and exhausting before, became fun and manageable when shared with others. Sandi and Greg had to learn to compromise on several of their ideas, but the result, after almost five years, has been a testimony to shared vision, co-creation and love-in-action. There are also several community projects, which generate income and all share in the work as well as in the benefit.

"It's completely different from what we had envisaged, and we've had to change our ideas about ownership and control," admits Sandi, "But, somehow, it really works very well and we're happy, healthy and have plenty of leisure time to enjoy this beautiful place in which we find ourselves. Now the community is considering purchasing the adjacent piece of land and providing an opportunity for another ten families to join us. And so we grow in love and in scope," she enthused. *"And, somehow, as we listen to our hearts, we also find ourselves listening to the rhythms and harmonies of our environment and everything just seems to work out really well for us."*

Sandi and Greg's story had provided me with much food for thought. If the Green Lady was able to appear in dreams, what could be her true nature, I wondered. Now I was even more anxious than ever to meet her for myself.

CHAPTER 5
THE CHANGELING

I was enjoying a late lunch of grilled calamari, accompanied by a glass of sparkling wine, in a small local bistro to celebrate the conclusion of a successful interview when I noticed the exquisitely fine watercolours of various indigenous plants and animals adorning the walls. Getting up to take a closer look at a glorious depiction in striking shades of amber and gold of a caracal greeting the sunrise, I was entranced by the delicacy and detailing of the brushwork. The combination of fine ink lines and vivid watercolours was quite striking and very unusual. I was leaning in to try and make out the artist's name at the bottom of the painting when a voice from behind my left shoulder informed me that, "*It's a local artist. Gorgeous, aren't they?*" Turning around, I encountered the owner of the restaurant smiling at me.

"*I have rarely seen such an exquisite combination of ink drawing and brushwork and, as for the colours...*" I lifted my eyebrows and smiled and shrugged for emphasis.

The restaurateur nodded his agreement and said, "*The artist is in her eighties, can you believe! She and her sister have lived in a little cottage at the edge of the forest since their youth. They're an institution in this town. If you're interested, I could give you their number and you could pay them a visit to view some more of the paintings. It would definitely be worth your while – they've got plenty of fascinating stories to tell.*" Well, as you can imagine, the ears of this inveterate story-magpie certainly pricked up at that!

And, so it was that two days later I coaxed my ancient, temperamental car down a potholed dirt road to visit the Judson sisters at Wisteria Cottage, their sanctuary and the final smallholding on the road, right at the very edge of the forest. Climbing out of my car, I was instantly knocked to the ground by an enormous, shaggy, boisterous dog of indeterminate breed. *"Petal, how very inhospitable of you! Stand down, girl!"* A clear, high-pitched voice, softly blanketed in gentle mirth, wafted down the overgrown, flower-adorned garden path. Looking up from my rather undignified sprawl on the dusty ground, I encountered a dumpy, twinkly little lady with bright, mischievous pale-blue eyes and a fluffy halo of silver candy-floss adorning her head. Petal, completely unabashed at her scolding, proceeded to enthusiastically lick my face, her tail furiously wagging and thumping my car door rather alarmingly as she did so. In an attempt to salvage at least a modicum of dignity, I pushed Petal aside and hoisted myself off the ground, wiping my hand on my trousers before introducing myself as Peter Allen, journalist and would-be author.

"I'm Emily Judson," reciprocated the lady, who appeared even smaller once I was vertical. *"Please come inside and meet Angela."*

The cottage was, rather comfortingly, exactly what one would have expected to be the taste of two single ladies of that vintage, featuring a preponderance of porcelain figurines, nestling on frilly, crocheted doilies and an abundance of pastel-coloured floral prints. I was directed to sit on a delicate-looking, over-stuffed chair sporting a needlepoint depiction of some rather startlingly unnatural blooms. I lowered myself somewhat gingerly, uncertain whether the chair would be able to bear my weight. Glancing around the room, I briefly imagined the devastation that Petal could effect on its delicate femininity, but my fears were assuaged when the dog was lovingly, but firmly, instructed to remain outside. *"I'll make us some tea,"* said Emily and then, as she was leaving the room, *"Ah, here's Angela. Come and entertain Mr. Allen, Sweetie, whilst I arrange some refreshments."*

I struggled out of the embrace of my rickety, overstuffed chair and turned around to meet the intense, icy-blue stare of a fey, otherworldly creature, who glided across the floral carpet with unconscious and ageless grace to grasp my outstretched hand in both of her angular, painfully cold, fine-boned hands. She was delicately made and carried her close-shorn head, with its prominent bones, like a dancer. Her clothing was severe and utterly without adornment or artifice. A greater contrast to her comfortable, mothering, self-consciously feminine sister would be hard to find. Angela lowered herself with ease and natural poise into an upright wooden chair and I settled, with considerably less grace, into my own uncomfortable seating.

"So, Mr. Allen, you are a story-teller," Angela said in a soft, breathy voice, *"But what, I wonder, is your own story?"* She had a gaze that made me feel immediately, and very deeply, seen; seen with all of my strengths and weaknesses, secrets, foibles and follies. I had just finished sketching for Angela the outline of my book when Emily arrived with the tea tray. Shortly, we were settled with a cup of tea and a piece of Emily's delicious, home-made, lemon cake each, which Angela proceeded to crumble onto her plate, her eyes never once leaving my face. Apropos of nothing, Angela suddenly blurted out, her gaze never once wavering, *"Emily, you may tell Mr. Allen our story. I will be in my studio,"* and then, abruptly, she

abandoned her tea and cake and drifted out of the room. I was left under no illusion as to who called the shots in Wisteria Cottage!

"*Well, then, let's have a nice chat, shall we?*" said Emily cosily and so that is exactly what we did...

Emily and Angela's mother, Enid, lost her childhood sweetheart during action of the Sixth South African Armoured Division in Italy in 1943. Their father, Nigel Judson, had seen his own fair share of action in North Africa and had lost a foot in the second battle of Al Alamein in 1942. He spent the rest of the war back in South Africa, doing an intellectually unchallenging administrative job whilst he recovered his strength and health and learned to use the prosthesis with which he had been fitted. During this time he met Enid, who was a typist in the office in which he worked and they were married in 1946. Nigel had been trained as an engineer and so, after the war, he and Enid relocated to Johannesburg where he gained lucrative employment as an engineer in the construction business. Emily was born a year later. It was an extremely difficult birth and, due to complications, Enid and Nigel were informed that there would be no further children. Enid took the news very badly and she suffered through years of depression, in which she gradually withdrew from the world. Emily learned very early on to be self-sufficient which, as it turned out, would be the perfect training for what lay ahead in her life.

When Emily was eight, she was sent to stay with her maternal grandmother for two weeks whilst her mother and father took a holiday in the forested mountains of Knysna. They stayed in a small, secluded cottage on the edge of the forest and swam daily in a rock pool fed by crystal-clear mountain streams. When her parents came to fetch her from her grandmother's house, it was immediately apparent to Emily that something had changed for her mother. The quiet, listless, pale mother she had always known had been replaced by a bright, vivacious, energetic stranger. It seemed as if the holiday had had a remarkably rejuvenating effect on her mother and the house was a much brighter, happier place after that, especially when, two months later, it was confirmed that Enid was, miraculously, pregnant. Their lives were now filled with joy and purpose as the family prepared themselves for the birth of their miracle baby. Emily was absolutely over-the-moon with excitement that she would be gaining a little sister (never once did she doubt that it would indeed be a sister). It seemed that her quiet, sad and lonely early childhood had taken a significant turn for the better.

Angela arrived in the world with relative ease and was a quiet, good baby with huge emerald-green eyes and a thick shock of curly, auburn hair. Enid jokingly called Angela her changeling baby, because never before had such vivid colouring been seen on either side of the family. For a short while all were blissfully happy in the Judson household. But, very gradually, Enid became aware that there was something not quite right about her youngest child. Angela was simply too quiet. She didn't babble as other babies did and had still not spoken a single word by the age of three. She refused to make eye contact, had never been seen to smile and turned away from all human touch. By four she had developed the distressing habit of crouching with her face turned to the wall and incessantly rocking backwards and forwards whilst tapping her fingers against her ears and making an unearthly, high-pitched, crooning noise. She didn't play with her toys, instead preferring to obsessively line them up in a specific order known only to herself. Any change to her routine or in her environment would bring on hours of incessant rocking, tapping and crooning.

Angela started disappearing from the house and would often be found only several, panic-filled, hours later, staring up into the canopy of a tree or wandering amongst the trees on an open plot of land close to the family home. Over time, Emily came to know Angela's favourite places and could usually find her within half an hour or so of her absence being noticed. It soon became clear that Emily was the only person who could calm Angela down. The little girl simply turned away from her mother and from everyone else.

Enid was devastated and gradually she too withdrew from both of her children and sank back into the depression which had characterized the years after Emily's birth. On Angela's sixth birthday, her mother crashed her car into a tree and never returned from the hospital. Angela didn't even seem to notice the absence of her mother. Nigel withdrew, broken-hearted, into his work during the day and his study at night and so the care of Angela fell to Emily. She left school at sixteen and devoted her time and energy to caring for her sister. Various family members attempted to intervene in order to prevent what they viewed as Emily throwing her life away to care for Angela. Others tried to convince Nigel to get Angela institutionalized, but Emily was so vehemently opposed to that idea and so clearly happy and fulfilled to be taking care of her sister that gradually the voices were silenced. As Emily herself told me, "I've always known that Angela was extremely special and so she deserved the very best love and care that I *could give her. It was my role, my responsibility, but also my pleasure and privilege to do so."*

When Emily was twenty-six and Angela was seventeen, Nigel was killed by a falling metal girder on a building site. The inheritance he left his daughters would be sufficient to provide them with a modest independence for life and Nigel's insurance payout was enough for them to purchase a small home. Emily decided that they would move out of the city and to the small town of Knysna, where her mother had briefly been so happy, which had directly resulted in the birth of her beloved sister. She purchased a small cottage on the edge of the forest and they settled down to a quiet, modest lifestyle.

The girls had been living in their new home for less than a month when Angela disappeared, as was her habit, but for the first time in many years Emily was really anxious. She had no idea of where Angela would go and there was the entire forest for her to get lost in – how was she ever going to find her sister again? In a complete panic, she rushed out of the cottage without her coat, leaving the door open in her haste to find her sister. Some instinct had her running down the path that led directly into the forest, repeatedly calling her sister's name. A tense and anxious half-hour ensued as Emily ran this-way-and-that, blindly following every little forest path and animal track she encountered in her panic to find her sister before some real harm befell her. Finally, a massive Yellowwood tree marked the end of the narrow animal track she had been following and Emily stepped out into a clearing in the forest, where she beheld the most astonishing sight.

Praise be, there was Angela, and seemingly unharmed! But, she was not alone. She was holding both the hands and gazing into the eyes of a very tall, slender, green woman, whose cascading dark-green hair barely cloaked her naked body, which was shocking enough to Emily. That Angela was actually choosing to touch someone and make eye contact was almost a stranger sight than her otherworldly companion. But, what happened next was even more incredible. Emily watched in amazement as, for the very first time, she witnessed sounds emerging from her sister's mouth. But, what sounds! Soft chirps and whirrs and buzzes and clicks issued in a constant stream and were answered in kind by similar sounds from the green woman. As they thus communicated, an enormous flock of tiny Cape White Eye birds descended upon them, settling on their heads and arms and shoulders and joining in the chorus of chirping and twittering. A pair of Orioles alighted on a nearby branch and broke into exquisite song, followed shortly by the arrival of countless other songbirds to add their voices to the exquisitely joyful cacophony. As Angela lifted her head back and closed her eyes to relish the song, Emily audibly gasped in wonderment at the sight before her. And then the Green Lady looked directly at Emily and it was clear that her presence had been noted from the very beginning. The Lady put her finger to her lips and Emily knew that she was to remain very still and to simply observe the magical spectacle unfolding before her eyes.

Angela and the Lady recommenced their otherworldly communication and this time they added a strange, high-pitched humming sound to the mix. Before Emily's delighted eyes, a hundred, no a thousand, multicoloured butterflies descended upon the Angela and the green woman in the forest glade. As a large, orange butterfly alit on the very tip of Angela's nose, Emily heard a sound that she had never dreamt to hear Angela make... a giggle, which developed into a chuckle and then evolved into peals of delighted, tinkling merriment. And, as the laughter erupted from Angela's upturned face, white blossoms appeared like drifts of confetti in the air above her, and Angela and the Lady began to twirl, holding hands as they spun faster and faster, enveloped in a riotous whirlwind of laughter and wild, swirling petals. Tears of joy and gratitude streamed down Emily's cheeks as she observed her sister's ecstatic reunion with what she recognized was Angela's kin, in a way that she would never be. At that realization Emily suddenly knew that she didn't belong there in the clearing and so, after one final glance at the entrancing scene before her, she turned and made her way back out of the forest and to her lonely home.

That night Emily crawled into her bed with a heavy heart, filled with a deep, aching void of emptiness and yearning. She knew that she would probably never see her sister again and it was as if the centre had dropped out of her life. Her very reason for being had disappeared, but she knew that she could not begrudge her sister the only real happiness she had ever experienced.

Emily awoke the following morning to the feel of warm lips kissing her cheek and a soft voice, saying the same thing over-and-over again. *"Emmie, wake up, I've returned."* Emily's eyes popped open in fright and, yes, indeed, there was Angela, standing right there at the side of her bed. *"I've returned, Emmie, I've returned to you,"* Angela repeated and Emily felt tears of gratitude and love welling up and spilling over to drench her cheeks and the pillow. As she sat up and stretched out her arms to her sister, Emily suddenly noticed something that made her heart beat very fast. Angela's eyes had changed colour; instead of the startling emerald-green they had always been, they were now the softest, palest blue, just like Emily's own. It seemed as if Emily's sister truly had returned to her at last.

CHAPTER 6
THE WARNING

I was idly flicking through the local Knysna newspaper whilst waiting for my takeaway pizza when a headline caught my eye: **"SUSPECTED HOUSEBREAKER FOUND WANDERING ON MOUNTAIN ROAD IN STATE OF SHOCK"**. Well, that certainly sounded like an intriguing story, so I settled down to read the full article.

It appeared that a Zimbabwean illegal alien, Tariro Manyika, had been found wandering on a steep, forested mountain road in a severe state of shock. He was incoherent and babbling and was nearly run over by a local farmer. The farmer, who suspected Mr. Manyika of being intoxicated at the time and also of potentially being involved in several break-ins that had occurred in the area over the past few months, drove Mr. Manyika to the local police station, where he was placed in a holding cell for the night. Initial screening failed to find any alcohol or drugs in his bloodstream. The following day, the body of another Zimbabwean man, known only as Simba, was found by local children, lying beside the river, close to a popular swimming hole at the bottom of a steep, forested gorge. Significantly, this was over 300 meters directly below the road on which Mr. Manyika had been apprehended the previous day. It was unclear whether these two cases were linked, although Mr. Manyika had been known to be living with Mr. Cashmore Zimunya, who was the putative employer of Simba, at the time of his death. Both cases were still under investigation.

Over the next few days I followed the story, interviewing the farmer who had found the suspect, the arresting police officers, the detectives assigned to the case and several other landowners in the area who had been victim to housebreaks over the past few months. Eventually, due to a contact within the police department, I was able to interview Mr. Manyika himself in a holding cell, where he was awaiting deportation back to Zimbabwe. This interview provided the most intriguing detail of all. The story that emerged was strange, to say the very least and, due to circumstances, there remain several inexplicable details, which will probably never be resolved. Below is my attempt to create a coherent picture of what actually happened in the months leading up to the events described in the newspaper article. In places I have had to patch up the holes in the story with some creative narrative of my own.

Tariro Manyika illegally crossed the border between South Africa and Zimbabwe during the dry season of June 2014. As he did not have the money to bribe officials at the Beitbridge border post, he crossed the crocodile-infested Limpopo River and crawled through a gap in the border fence at night. Over the next few weeks he walked and hitchhiked where possible, eventually making his way to Knysna where his cousin, Tinashe Nandoro, had been living in an informal settlement on the outskirts of Knysna for several months and had married a local South African woman, which had granted him legal status.

Tinashe and Tariro had grown up together in the rural village of Nkalanje, in Zimbabwe's arid South Matabeleland Province. The village had experienced severe food shortages due to an extended period of drought and Tinashe, who was two years older than Tariro and had always been bolder and more confident, decided to leave the village to seek his fortune in South Africa. Before he left, he promised Tariro that he would always provide a home and a living for his younger cousin. At the time that Tanashe left Zimbawe, the boys' grandmother, who had always been a stabilizing influence on the family was still alive. But when she died ten months later and Tariro's hopes of finding a suitable bride in his village were dashed due to the ever-increasing poverty of his family, he decided to follow his cousin to South Africa. He had received word that Tanashe had found work, a wife and a suitable place to stay in the small coastal town of Knysna and so it was that, with great hope, Tariro bid his family farewell and began the long journey to the land of milk and honey to the south of Zimbabwe. He was twenty years old, strong and healthy and full of hope and optimism that he would make his fortune in South Africa and return to his country a hero. After all, did his very name not signify hope and a belief in a brighter future?

When Tariro finally arrived in Knysna almost a month later, his optimism considerably dimmed, he was painfully thin, his clothes were ragged and filthy and his shoes were full of holes. To his great disappointment, Tanashe's home in the settlement was no more than a shack built of rusty corrugated iron sheets and cardboard and his much-touted job was as a casual labourer in a local sawmill. But the cousins were overjoyed to see each other again and, after he had rested and regained his strength, Tariro set about trying to find a job. This proved to be extremely difficult, as he was an illegal alien without a valid work permit and most employers simply sent him away upon discovering this fact. He was able to find the odd day job here and there, doing hard labour, under poor working conditions, for very little pay. In addition, he experienced increasing hostility from South Africans who resented the fact that he, as an illegal alien, was taking jobs that should, by rights, be theirs, especially since employers were able to get away with paying the Zimbabweans and other aliens far less than the locals. A month in, and Tariro was barely making enough money to pay for his own food and a small amount of rental to Tanashe for the meagre accommodation provided by his shack.

And then the rains arrived. Knysna is one of the highest rainfall areas in South Africa and it can often rain for days, or even weeks, on end. The constant drip of water and the icy winter winds howling through the gaps between the corrugated iron sheets of Tanashe's hut made life miserable for all three inhabitants of the little shack. After a month or two, Tanashe's wife, Innocence, who was four months pregnant at the time, began to complain that Tariro was taking up too much space in their small shack and that the rental he paid did not even cover the cost of his food. The situation was dire and Tariro really didn't know what he should do. This was not at all what he had envisaged back in Zimbabwe and he seriously considered leaving South Africa to return home.

Tariro's optimism was at its lowest ebb when he met Cashmore on a Sunday afternoon at the local shebeen[2]. He was not in the habit of frequenting the shebeen, nor did he have the money to pay for much beer, but Innocence's complaints had finally started to sway Tanashe's opinion in her

---

2   A shebeen is an unlicensed drinking establishment, often found in informal settlements in South Africa.

favour and, for the first time ever, Tariro felt that his cousin would actually prefer it if he were to return to Zimbabwe. He decided to spend the afternoon away from the shack, and so he entered the local drinking place with the intention of nursing a single beer for a couple of hours so as to give Tanashe and Innocence some time alone together.

Upon entering the shebeen, Tariro noticed a very sharply dressed man, surrounded by a bevy of beautiful women, hanging on his every word. Tariro knew that he was beneath the notice of such an important man and was, therefore, extremely surprised when the man approached him a short while later and introduced himself as Cashmore, the owner of the shebeen. Tariro had heard of Cashmore Zimunya, who was notorious in the informal settlement and rumoured to be involved in various nefarious and illegal activities. But the man that Tariro met that day was really friendly and welcoming and he provided Tariro with a constant supply of free beer and introduced him to the beautiful women in his entourage, who also went out of their way to make Tariro feel welcome. This was balm to the soul of a lonely, homesick village boy.

By late afternoon Tariro was nicely tipsy and had regaled Cashmore with his life story. Cashmore insisted that Tariro stay rent-free on the sleeper couch in the back room of his shebeen, which sounded like a fantastic deal, as the shebeen was properly built and did not leak in the rain. Tariro slept warm and dry that night for the first time in several weeks, and the following day his spirits were raised even further as Cashmore told him that he had a small job for him to do. All he had to do was to accompany one of Cashmore's men to collect some money owed, and for the afternoon's work he would be paid the equivalent of two day's normal wages.

Tariro did experience a small twinge of concern, especially when he met Simba, the man he was to accompany that afternoon. Simba was a very large and muscular man who communicated only in grunts, monosyllables or quick, impatient gestures of his head and hands. But Cashmore kept smiling at Tariro and so he pushed his worries aside and climbed into the back of Cashmore's car. Cashmore drove several kilometres up a steep, mountainous dirt road and then dropped Simba and Tariro off a couple of hundred meters before the first homestead of a small settlement high in the mountains at the edge of the forest.

"*Now, listen boys,*" warned Cashmore, "*Get in-and-out as quickly as possible. Split up when you're done and make your own way back down the mountain, staying out of sight. Tariro, do exactly what Simba tells you to do and you'll be fine.*" With a final wolfish grin at Tariro, Cashmore slammed the car door shut, turned the vehicle around and sped off down the mountain. Tariro felt a sharp spike of fear. He was now sure that he had made the biggest mistake of his life, but a quick glance over at Simba's scowling face and menacing bulk informed him, in no uncertain terms, that he had no choice but to go through with the job and hope for the best.

Simba and Tariro walked past several homesteads, staying out of sight of the occupants of two cars that passed them on the dirt road. Finally, they reached a smallholding that appeared to be their destination. There was a small, wooden house a couple of hundred metres away, at the end of a long, winding driveway. Simba indicated, with a jerk of his head, that Tariro was to approach the house. When they reached their destination, Simba told Tariro to wait outside, keep watch and to alert him if anyone approached. The door to the house was unlocked and Simba entered whilst Tariro waited outside, his knees knocking and his heart pounding with fear. What on Earth had he gotten himself into? He cursed and berated himself but remained waiting outside the door and, within ten minutes, Simba emerged with two small, opaque plastic bags, one of which he gave to Tariro, with instructions to put it inside his shirt and to close his jacket. Then the two men rapidly departed down the driveway. Simba told Tariro to walk back down the mountain the way they had come, keeping out of sight of any vehicles or people he might encounter and then to go straight to the shebeen and hand the packet over to Cashmore. *"Don't open the packet and don't fuck this up,"* was his parting shot, delivered with a menacing scowl. Tariro hastened away, not lingering to see which direction Simba would take down the mountain, but rather feeling extremely grateful to remove himself from the other man's presence.

The trip down the mountain was uneventful and, within two hours, Tariro was back at the shebeen where he handed the package over to Cashmore, who pocketed it without giving it a second glance and then instructed one of his women to pour a beer for *"my young friend"*. He handed Tariro a roll of banknotes, which Tariro pocketed, thinking as he did so of the many, many hours of hard labour that he would have had to have endured to have earned the same amount of cash.

Two weeks, and several small jobs, later and Tariro was far less reluctant than he had been before. He had started to become accustomed to having a bit of cash and was enjoying the warm, dry accommodation and the company of Cashmore's ever-willing and hospitable lady-friends. He told himself that he wasn't really stealing, just running extremely well-paid errands for his new friend, Cashmore. Tanashe, who had encountered him outside the shebeen, had warned Tariro that he was getting himself into big trouble. *"Cashmore is a snake, cousin. You are getting into some deep waters here. Be very sure that you are able to swim,"* he cautioned. But Tariro laughed off his concerns and told him to worry about his wife and his unborn son instead.

The following morning Cashmore told Tariro that he had another job for him that would be worth double what he had been paid up to that point. He and Simba would be returning to the mountain settlement to, *"settle a debt"*, as Cashmore put it.

That afternoon Cashmore dropped the men off at the same point as before. This time their destination was a large, modern farmhouse right at the edge of the settlement and bordering on the indigenous forest. The road curving into the property was demarked by a low retaining wall at the very edge of a steep, forested gorge. Just outside the farmhouse, Simba reached into his jacket pocket and handed Tariro a sharp-looking knife and grabbed from his other pocket a gun. Tariro gasped in fear and surprise, but a fierce glare from Simba informed him that he should shut up if he valued his own life. Simba cautiously opened the back door of the farmhouse (Tariro wondered if everybody in this neighbourhood left their doors unlocked!) and stepped inside, gesturing at Tariro to stay behind him and to watch his back. They entered a large, comfortably-appointed living room and Simba headed straight for an open door leading off of this room. Following in his wake, Tariro discovered that the door led to a home office, but noticed, to his horror, that there was a man sitting at a desk reading some papers, his back to the door.

Simba slipped silently in through the door, gesturing to Tariro to follow him and to quietly close the door behind him. Tariro watched Simba grab the man around the neck from behind and whisper fiercely in his ear in English, *"Shut up and do exactly as I say if you want to live!"* The man nodded in terror and Tariro watched in horrified fascination as Simba got the man to unlock the safe and remove several large wads of cash and numerous gold coins, as well as a couple of thin folders. Simba placed the coins and cash in a plastic bag, which he pocketed, and then handed the folders to Tariro, who tucked them into his shirt, as he had been instructed to do in the past. Then Simba handed Tariro several cable ties and told him to securely tie the man's hands and feet to the arms and legs of his chair. Simba himself stuffed a large wad of fabric into the man's mouth and taped his mouth shut with duct tape. Then he grabbed the man's hair and pulled his head back. The man's eyes widened and rolled back in terror as Simba whispered into his ear again, *"Just stay here quietly for a little while and your wife and children will be fine. Cause a fuss and we'll be back for them next, OK?"* The man briefly nodded his head, perspiration rolling down his cheeks. Giving another sharp yank to the man's hair for good measure, Simba indicated that Tariro should leave, and within ten minutes they were back on the road again. *"You know what to do. Don't you dare fuck up!"* he spat at Tariro and turned to leave in the opposite direction.

Tariro was in a state of absolute terror. Somehow he had been able to hide from himself the true nature of what he had been doing up to this point. But it had all suddenly become very, very real indeed, and he knew that Tanashe had been right – he was in extremely deep waters and he was no longer sure that he would ever be able to swim out. He sprinted all the way down that mountain and back to the shebeen, fortunately not encountering a single soul on the mountain road. Upon entering the shebeen, he just about threw the folders at Cashmore, and even the wad of cash that he received for his role in the afternoon's activities did not make him feel any better. As soon as he could, he excused himself and went to his room to lie in his bed with his head beneath the covers, shivering as if in the grip of a fever.

Eventually, after some hours, the pounding of Tariro's heart abated and he fell into a deep, disturbed sleep. He was plagued by dreams of monsters and demons, grabbing him and biting chunks out of his flesh. Then, an immensely tall, terrifying green woman, with blinding yellow light shining out of her eyes, pinioned him with her gaze and he discovered, to his horror, that his limbs were paralysed. As he watched, helpless, she snarled at him and he saw enormous, sharp, yellow teeth lengthening in her mouth. She lifted her hands and cruel, yellow talons split through the green skin and curved into claws. Then she bent forward onto all fours and he realized that the green woman had changed into a massive, tawny leopard, with muscles rippling beneath her spotted pelt, ready to pounce. It was Nehanda[3], who was possessed by the mhondoro or lion spirit, and she was absolutely furious with

---

3   Nehanda Charwe Nyakasikana (1840–1898) was a spirit medium of the Shona people, who was reputed to have been inhabited by the spirit of the lion, or the mhondoro. She inspired an uprising against the British colonisation of what is now called Zimbabwe. She was eventually captured and executed by the British. Clearly Tariro mistakenly identified the Green Lady as Nehanda, inhabited by the mhondoro. This was one of the many stories told to Tariro by his grandmother when he was a little boy.

him. She wanted revenge. She wanted to kill him! And then she pounced...

Tariro awoke with a start, drenched in perspiration and screaming in terror. He was absolutely sure that the mhondoro would find and kill him to avenge the people he had harmed through his actions of the past few weeks. All of the stories that his grandmother had told him about the vengeful mhondoro during his childhood were about to come true. He was terrified and he felt more vulnerable and alone than he had ever been in his entire life.

Tariro kept a very low profile over the next few weeks, taking particular care to stay out of Cashmore's way. This wasn't too difficult as Cashmore was rather distracted. Simba had been apprehended on his way down the mountain after the last job he had done with Tariro, and the cash and coins on his person had been discovered by the police, which had led to his arrest and incarceration. Cashmore had had to bribe a police officer to secure Simba's release and, during the time that it took to affect all of this, Tariro saw a completely different side to the erstwhile charming Cashmore. He screamed and shouted and raged about the shebeen, overturning furniture and smashing glasses and bottles. The verbal lambasting that Simba endured when he was finally released by the police was truly terrifying to witness. Tariro was sick to his stomach as he knew that what he needed to tell Cashmore would aggravate his employer's mood even further.

But, when Tariro finally gathered his courage to tell Cashmore that he was leaving for Zimbabwe and that he could no longer work for him, Cashmore merely smiled a thin, cold and terrifying smile, *"Don't be a fool, little boy. Of course you aren't leaving and of course you will still work for me. If you don't, you will very quickly find yourself in prison, and the* police in possession of all the evidence they need to put your sweet little black ass away for armed robbery for many years to come. Now, tomorrow you and Simba will finish the job you botched up last time. I need you to find certain items that you missed the last time round."

And that, it seemed, was that. Tariro decided that he had no choice but to do the job the following day, as Cashmore would now be watching him very closely. But tomorrow night, after the job was done and Cashmore was once again sure of Tariro's loyalty, he would sneak away and get back home to Zimbabwe as fast as he possibly could. He now realised that he was completely out of his depth and he longed for the simple, uncomplicated life that he had enjoyed back home in his village.

The following morning saw Simba and Tariro crouching behind the low retaining wall that separated the road to the farmhouse from the steep gorge below, watching the farmer and his family slowly disappear down the road in their SUV in a cloud of dust. As Tariro stood up, he noticed a flash of green light to his left and, turning in that direction, he was horrified to notice the green woman from his nightmare standing right behind Simba, who was facing Tariro. "*What are you staring at, boy?*" Simba snarled, "*Let's go, we've got work to do.*" Gaining absolutely no response from the wildly staring Tariro and, following the direction of the younger man's eyes, Simba slowly turned around, only to encounter the woman, who was growing teeth and claws, just as she had in Tariro's nightmare.

"*What the..!*" gasped Simba, his eyes widening in terror as the woman crouched down, rapidly becoming a massive, powerful leopard, ready to pounce. "*Whoever you are, just stay the fuck away from me!*" Simba screamed, stepping backwards away from the beast, just as she finally pounced. And then Simba and the mhondoro became a blur before Tariro's eyes as they rolled through the brush and then plummeted down the steep gorge, disappearing into the dense undergrowth hundreds of metres below, accompanied by Simba's final, prolonged and agonised scream, which abruptly ended... to be replaced by a deathly silence.

Tariro then completely lost his grip on his sanity. He put his hands to his head and began yanking at his hair and making soft, keening noises as he sweated and blubbered, snot running down his face. He sank to his knees and clutched at the retaining wall as if it represented his only salvation. Then, suddenly, he jumped to his feet, leapt over the wall and began sprinting down the road at top speed for a few hundred meters, only to stop dead in the middle of the road and begin walking in circles, sobbing and keening again as he beat his fists against his head. At this point he was almost run over by the local farmer, who took him down to the police station.

As no incriminating evidence had been found on Tariro's person, the only crime of which he could conclusively be found guilty, after several days of questioning and investigation, was that of being an illegal alien in South Africa. After some months of detention in various holding cells, both in Knysna and in the closest city, George, Tariro was eventually deported back to Zimbabwe. Within a few days of being dropped at the border post, he was back in his village, his thirst for adventure completely quenched, hopefully for good.

Some weeks after writing up this story, I was finally able to interview the farmer who had been robbed at gunpoint by Simba and Tariro. His cash and gold coins, which had been found in Simba's possession, had eventually been returned to him by the police and his only loss had been copies of his will and a few other legal documents, which were of no value to anyone else. During our discussions, it transpired that Cashmore had, some years previously, worked for, and been fired by, this farmer, due to certain, undisclosed illegal activities, which the farmer chose not to report to the authorities. However, the farmer still held incriminating evidence on Tariro's ex-employer. It was these incriminating documents that Cashmore had wanted to retrieve, as well as to exercise a desire for revenge upon his erstwhile employer.

Just as I was leaving, the farmer turned to me, a small smile curving his lips, and remarked, "*I asked her for protection, you know.*" Seeing my bemused look, he elaborated, "*After the first robbery. I asked the Lady for protection.*"

"*The Lady? Have you encountered her before?*" I enquired, a tremor in my voice betraying my excitement.

"*Oh, yes!*" he smiled again, clearly enjoying my response to his disclosure. "*I've met her several times over the years, the frequency increasing as I started moving towards more organic farming methods and particularly when I installed some bee hives on my farm. She makes an appearance every now and then to offer me some advice or to acknowledge some improvement in my farming methods. After the first robbery I called on her to protect my farm and my family. And... I reckon she obliged!*"

The mystery surrounding the Green Lady only seemed to deepen, the more stories about her I encountered. Now, more than ever, I wished that I too could meet her and discover who she was and what motivated her appearances and her actions.

Chapter 7
Peak Experience

Before coming to Knysna, I had heard from a friend, who was an enthusiastic amateur diver, that the shipwreck of the Paquita in the Knysna estuary was a very interesting and popular dive site.

The Paquita was a German ship which was purported to have been deliberately sunk by its captain for insurance fraud purposes off the Eastern side of the Knysna heads in 1903. The Knysna Heads are comprised of two magnificent sea cliffs that guard the entrance to the Knysna estuary. I was told that divers could descend up to sixteen meters deep to explore the ship, which was in good condition and that there was apparently a wealth of marine life to be viewed. There was even the possibility of viewing the endangered Knysna seahorse, which is indigenous to the Knysna estuary. As I had never dived before, I decided to complete a one-day resort dive course to see whether I enjoyed the sport, as I would have to complete my first open water certificate before being allowed to dive down to view the Paquita.

Sadly, it very rapidly became clear to me that I would have to give up on my diving ambitions, as I experienced a severe sense of claustrophobia when using the breathing apparatus and I also found it virtually impossible to equalize the pressure in my sinuses, probably due to a chronic sinusitis condition that I had suffered from my entire life. I was extremely disappointed, but the diving expedition had one unexpected upside – I met Ken Brady, who was to supply a truly inspiring story for my book.

I was sitting in the dive shop at the Knysna Heads waiting for my dive instructor to appear, when a small, wiry man with a shaggy mop of shoulder-length, curly black hair strode purposefully into the shop, clad only in a wetsuit and sneakers. From his conversation with the dive shop owner, which I couldn't help but overhear, it was very clear that he was an experienced diver. His own compressor was giving problems and so he had come to the shop to have his tanks filled with air for the dives he had planned for the day. Whilst the shop owner was busy filling the tanks, the man sat down next to me and opened a can of iced tea, which he thirstily downed. I introduced myself and then remarked, *"Sounds like you've got some serious dives planned for today."*

And that was all that was required to encourage my diminutive friend to begin expounding upon his favourite topic: the endangered Knysna seahorse. His name was Ken Brady and he was a marine biologist from the University of Cape Town, who was staying in Knysna for two years to complete the practical requirements for his PhD project on the seahorse. His dives were aimed at studying the distribution and population densities of the seahorse in various habitats, on different vegetation and under various conditions. I have always enjoyed listening to well-informed and single-minded people speaking about their passions and so I listened intently as he shared with me some fascinating information about the endangered seahorse.

Sea horses are actually fish, possessing both fins and swim bladders. They have horse-like heads and anchor themselves to underwater vegetation, where they wait for their prey. They have no stomachs and so must constantly graze on tiny fish, plankton or crustaceans. The Knysna seahorse is the only seahorse species that inhabits one of three different estuaries in the region (the Knysna, Keurbooms and Swartvlei estuaries) in areas with high vegetation cover. The limited range of this specific seahorse puts it at great risk of extinction, hence the efforts of Ken and others of his ilk. The fact that I found to be the most fascinating was that the seahorse males actually give birth to the babies! The female seahorse deposits her eggs into the male's pouch where they are fertilized and carried by the males until birth. Directly after the live birth, the female will deposit more eggs and the whole cycle begins again. Ken told me that the health of the Knysna seahorse population is an important indicator of estuary health. It is vital to understand the system in order to effectively manage and conserve it.

Ken paused suddenly in his monologue, as if realizing that he had perhaps somewhat overdone the impromptu lecture, and then he asked me what I was doing in town. Upon hearing about my book, he became even more excited and agitated than he had been when talking about the Knysna seahorse. He informed me that he had had an inexplicable, transformative experience a year earlier and said that he was certain that his story would be a potential candidate for my book. At that point my dive instructor finally arrived and Ken scrabbled in his wallet, from which he removed a crumpled and somewhat soiled business card, which he presented to me, saying, "*I'm available most evenings. Give me a call tonight?*" We shook hands and went our separate ways.

And so it was that the following Saturday evening, as Ken and I relaxed on the scruffy lounge suite in his somewhat Spartan apartment with a couple of beers, he told me his story.

Ken was the younger son of parents who were both school teachers. His older brother was popular and good at sports, but Ken had always been quiet, slightly geeky and far more interested in science than in social or sporting activities. He excelled in biology and mathematics at school and was a member of the debating society. Ken's parents were both highly intelligent, rational atheists and when Ken won a regional debating competition, in which he successfully upheld Nietzsche's contention that God was dead, his father told him that he was proud of him for the very first time. Ken's favourite book at this time was Richard Dawkins's bestseller, *The God Delusion*.

Ken elected to study a basic science degree at university. During his undergraduate years, he completed his first certificate in diving and became, for the first time in his life, hooked on an outdoors activity. He decided to combine his science with his passion for diving and so he selected marine biology as his post-graduate specialization, which eventually led to his PhD project on seahorses.

During the years of his studies, Ken maintained the perspective that the only rational, defendable position for a scientist, or indeed for any intelligent person, was that of atheism. In fact, an argument over the intellectual defensibility of agnosticism versus atheism was the reason for the break-up of his first serious relationship! *"Back then, I only believed in things that I could directly experience and confirm, with the application of incontrovertible proof and solid deductive reasoning, for myself,"* Ken told me. *"I had absolutely no patience or time for what I considered to be fuzzy, lazy thinking and self-delusion."*

"And now?" I asked, grabbing a couple more beers from the fridge.

"Now... now I'm not sure of anything any more," he grimaced, shrugging his shoulders. *"My father thinks I've lost my mind, but all I know is what I experienced, which was so incredibly powerful, so inexplicable that..."* he shook his head, as words failed him, taking a long swig of his beer. *"And I have absolutely no proof of anything whatsoever!"* he sighed, before proceeding to tell me the story of what had happened to him a year earlier.

Ken had planned a dive to visit the seagrass meadows around Leisure Isle, which is a small islet in the Knysna estuary, one early morning in spring. His aim was to study and document the distribution of specific vegetation in this part of the estuary. Everything went according to plan and soon he was drifting along at a depth of less than ten metres, taking notes on his underwater note pad and photographing the vegetation. *"The visibility was excellent and I got some solid work done,"* he recalled. *"I was just about to turn around to swim back to the shore when it happened."* At this point Ken got up and walked outside onto his small balcony with a distant view of the Knysna heads. I followed him, trying my best to be patient as he collected his thoughts and prepared to share his transformative experience. Ken's previous self-assured manner had evaporated and the story that emerged was related with much stammering and hesitation and punctuated with long silences and continuous head shaking. I have tried to summarise what he told me and present it in a clear and succinct fashion below.

Ken had just packed his notebook and camera into their respective pouches when a sudden, brilliant flash of bright green light caught his eye. Looking up, he was astounded to notice that the quality of the light underwater had dramatically changed. Suddenly the water looked like liquid gold, with tiny pinprick motes of bright white sparking in-and-out of existence. Wondering whether he had been under the water for longer than he had initially thought, Ken checked his air pressure gauge, but he still had more than enough oxygen to complete his dive. He checked the time on his diving watch so as to verify the amount of time he had spent underwater, and confirmed that this too was absolutely acceptable. Looking up again, he was struck by the brilliant intensity of a massive false plum anemone gently waving its tentacles in the current. He had noticed it earlier but now the colours almost hurt his eyes in their intensity. Even the extensive eelgrass meadows were almost unbearably luminous-green and the greenish-brown shaggy sea hare he glimpsed at his feet suddenly appeared to be miraculous and perfect in way he had never before experienced. In fact, looking around, he realized that absolutely everything he could see was almost unbearably intense in its perfect being-ness.

"What's happening to me? Could I be having an hallucination?" he wondered, but he wasn't diving nearly deep enough to be experiencing the influence of nitrogen narcosis and when he checked his air pressure again, the gauge confirmed that all was still well. Besides, he realized, he felt no fear or anxiety whatsoever, but rather a wonderful feeling of euphoria, a sense of expansion of the self, a feeling of connection and... yes, a feeling of all-encompassing love and well-being. And then, before Ken could even think to worry again about his safety underwater, he was completely overwhelmed by feelings and sensations of such magnitude that, even relating his experiences to me more than a year later caused him to sink down onto the chair as if his legs could no longer support his weight; copious tears streaming unheeded down his cheeks.

Suddenly, Ken the rationalist, the atheist, was having an experience which no amount of logical reasoning could possibly explain. He felt a powerful sense of unity, of connection with all that was around him; in fact, with all that was anywhere and everywhere. He knew, without a shadow of a doubt, that he shared one consciousness with the entire estuary and all of its inhabitants. He could sense the mudprawns and baitworms hiding beneath the sand and he discovered that he could choose to experience the world from the perspective of the tiny sandflat crabs climbing over the eelgrass leaves or from that of the fish swimming through it. Looking around, he realized that he could choose to view the world from any perspective whatsoever, including that of the seagrass limpets, the miniscule sea slugs, the oval-leafed saltweed, or even, he realized with a gasp, the entire estuary as one living, breathing, conscious organism.

As his perspective continued to expand, he suddenly knew, with absolute certainty, that he was one living, sentient being with an infinity of perspectives from which to choose. He realized that he could see through the water for as far as he wanted and could zoom in on the most intricate details of the tiniest creature or zoom out to view the world from a macro-perspective. He was One with all that is! Ken felt as if his heart was cracking open and tears began to run down his face, misting up his diving mask. Then, the diving mask became absolutely irrelevant as he felt himself expand even further until Ken disappeared altogether and he found himself residing deep within the heart of the God in whom he had never believed. He was One. He was Love.

An infinity later, Ken awoke once more to the limited perspective to which he had always been accustomed. He was back in his body in a diving suit, in an eelgrass meadow in the Knysna estuary. Clearing his mask, he looked down at his pressure gauge once more and was astounded to discover that he still had exactly the same amount of oxygen he had had since he had last checked. How could that be possible? Eons of time had elapsed in his experience, but somehow in the estuary time seemed to have stood still. He checked his watch to confirm that, indeed, no time at all had elapsed since he had decided to head for home.

Ken remained silent for a very long time until I asked him, *"How do you explain what happened to you?"*

"I simply have no words... no explanations," he replied. *"But I do know that I am irrevocably altered. I no longer believe that we cease to exist when we die. I retain the sense of being a part of a great whole, albeit just a faint echo of the feeling I had underwater. I feel like my life has meaning and purpose and that what I do, say and feel really matters."*

"It seems as if your experience has made the atheist religious," I feebly joked, feeling a bit out of my depth.

"No, not religious," he said, *"What I experienced that day could not possibly be encapsulated in the doctrines of any religion I have ever encountered. I simply cannot believe that the magnificence I connected with could possibly be described or understood by any traditional religion. It was a personal, mystical journey into the heart of God. What I do believe is that I am part of something far grander and more miraculous than anything I could ever have imagined in my widest*

dreams. We all are. It humbles me. It lifts me up and then throws me down onto my knees in gratitude and joy."

I had no idea of how to respond to Ken's effusion, but I knew that I too wanted to have such an experience. *"Why do you think that you had this experience, Ken?"* I asked, hoping that his answer might provide me with the means of procuring just such an experience for myself.

"Man, I don't know!" he rather disappointingly answered. *"I've done quite a bit of research and it seems that what I had was a peak experience. The psychologist, Abraham Maslow, did quite a bit of work on this phenomenon. There are those who believe that these experiences are delusions. But I find that I don't actually care what anyone else says or thinks about the topic. All I know is what I felt and experienced and I know that my life is forever changed. On the surface, nothing seems to have changed. I still go diving most days, I still write up my notes and take photos and publish my findings and work on my dissertation. But, underneath the mundane details, everything is different. I feel purposeful, I feel loved and I feel connected. But, most of all, I feel excitement and anticipation that someday, soon, I will be able to shift this current limited perspective that I now hold as Ken and once again hold the perspective that lies within the heart of God. That is what gives my life such meaning now."*

I left Ken's apartment with far more questions than answers. But his story certainly confirmed, yet again, that there was something about this special place that was transforming peoples' lives. In fact, the longer I resided there, the more I was beginning to feel its influence in my own life.

CHAPTER 8
WHO ARE YOU REALLY?

I met Christine whilst shopping at the local grocery store. We both reached for the same carton of free-range eggs, and then painfully bumped our heads as we withdrew, leading to profuse, simultaneous apologies. With her long, dark hair, bright, laughing, brown eyes and neat little body, Christine was exactly my type, and so I invited her to join me for a cup of coffee to apologise for injuring her. She must have found me somewhat interesting, as she agreed, but then inquired whether her sixteen-year old son, Gerry, could join us. At that, a lanky, surly-looking boy with a really unfortunate floppy hairstyle draped his arm around his mother with a somewhat proprietorial air. But any awkwardness dissipated as Christine and I drank a cup of coffee and shared a triple chocolate muffin and a laugh afterwards. Gerry played with his phone, rocking back on two legs of his chair and generally displaying all the signs of a normal teenager who wanted to dissociate himself from the boring adults in whose company he was forced to be.

Inevitably, Christine (or Chrissie for short) asked what it was that I was doing in Knysna and whilst I was explaining, I noticed that her son was listening most intently, in stark contrast to his previous attitude. When I had finished telling my story and Chrissie had asked all the normal and expected questions, Gerry leaned forward and said, *"Dude, if you want to hear a REAL story, you should speak to some guys at my school."*

"*Really? How so?*" I asked, trying to play it cool in the hope that he would reveal more.

"*Yeah man, some kids from my school went camping last Christmas holiday and something freaky happened to them. That should definitely be in your book,*" he affirmed. Well, of course, I was very aware that it would be tricky trying to get a story out of teenagers without coming across as either creepy or threatening to them. So I rapidly improvised a crafty plan, which would have the added benefit of currying favour with Christine.

"*Hey, Gerry, how would you like to be my assistant reporter on this story?*" I asked. "*You could interview the kids involved and then report back to me and we would develop the story together. If I can use the story in my book, I'll pay you for your time.*"

Gerry squinted at me for a moment. "*How much?*" he asked, and I knew I was in.

Over the next two weeks, Gerry interviewed all six of the teenagers who had been involved. He proved to be a very thorough and competent interviewer, albeit prone to hyperbole and over-dramatic statements. Below is the story that emerged.

During the previous December summer holiday, six tenth-grade students from the local high school had decided to camp overnight in the Knysna forest. The father of one of the boys, Terence (Terry) Parker, worked for SanParks, (South African National Parks) and so they were able to gain access to parts of the forest that were normally off limits to campers.

The father dropped the teenagers off in an isolated part of the forest at around four pm, with strict instructions to only build their fire in the designated fire pit and to refrain from damaging any plant or animal life. He told the boys that he would be back to fetch them at ten am the following morning. Terry's father, Cyril, did not believe in mollycoddling teenagers and thought that children needed to be exposed to Nature-in-the-raw in order to gain a proper appreciation for all that their hard-working parents provided for them.

Of course, the minute that Cyril's four wheel drive vehicle disappeared in a cloud of dust, the alcohol that the boys had been hiding in their backpacks made its appearance and the party got underway. Terry and David, a quiet, shy and eager-to-please boy, who had only been included in the expedition because he was the twin brother of Jack, the most popular boy in the group, set out to gather firewood so that they could cook their dinner. Jack and Sipho, another very popular boy and Jack's personal henchman, settled in for some serious drinking. By the time that Terry and David returned with armfuls of wood, Jack and Sipho were well on their way to becoming seriously plastered. The remaining two boys, John and Liam, who were also quite inebriated, were horsing around, chasing and throwing pinecones at each other.

"Guys, help me make this fire," Terry tried to bring proceedings back in order. "It's going to be dark soon and we'll need a fire to cook our food and to keep warm. Also, there are leopards and other predators hanging around in the forest and we need a fire to keep them at bay." This last comment was inspired, as it captured the imagination of John and Liam and so they helped the other two boys to make the fire; John cracking silly jokes the entire time. Jack and Sipho remained aloof, simply observing the fire-making activities and making serious inroads into the bottle of peach-flavoured vodka that Jack had liberated from beneath the frozen peas in his mother's freezer.

Before too long, the boys were roasting marshmallows around a roaring campfire and were soaking up some of the booze with potato crisps and dried beef. In time, as the coals became ready, the boys cooked their meat and engaged in further serious drinking and not-so-serious banter.

Then, just as the sun was beginning to set, Liam, who was a tall, weedy redhead with freckles and a sharp nose, said, *"Hey, guys, have any of you ever tripped before?"*

"Well, you tripped the other day when I tied your shoelaces together, you idiot!" crowed John, very pleased with his wit.

"So, I guess John's not interested in trying something new. Great, more for the rest of us," Liam leaned back against a stone and waited for the others to drag the story out of him.

"What are you talking about, man? Come on; don't leave us in suspense here. What have you got?" asked Sipho.

"Yeah, you tosser, spill the beans or stop hogging the limelight," grumbled Jack, who often found Liam's sly and insinuating ways irritating.

"Well, perhaps I'll just keep them all for myself then," sniffed Liam, not overly pleased with the way in which his secret had not played to his advantage, as anticipated.

"Get it from him, Sipho," drawled Jack and a very few short moments later, Sipho, who played prop on the first rugby team, had extracted from Liam's pocket a transparent bag of bright-red-and-white mushrooms, that looked like the typical toadstools from fairytales, and handed the bag to Jack.

"*What the hell is this?*" asked Jack, rather put out that Liam had been in possession of the mushrooms without him, Jack, being aware of it.

"*Hey, those are Amanita muscaria, or fly agaric,*" said Terry, whose father had educated his children well on the forest's fauna and flora.

"*You what...?*" spluttered John, giggling like an idiot. "*No man, you just made that up!*"

"*Seriously, guys, that stuff's dangerous. It causes heavy hallucinations,*" cautioned Terry.

"*Well, exactly! That's precisely why we're going to eat some shroomies tonight,*" crowed Liam, regaining some of his earlier advantage as he relished the attention he was getting.

"*That's a very bad idea, dude,*" said Terry, "*That stuff can kill you or you could have a seriously bad trip. You don't know how much you're getting in a dose!*"

"*What, are you, chicken? You don't have to have any, Mr. lick-arse head-boy-wannabe,*" sneered Liam, grabbing the bag back from Jack. "*Well, perfect, more for the rest of us, then. I found the shrooms, so I'll decide who gets what!*" The boys gathered around as Liam opened the bag and divided the mushrooms into five, more-or-less equal piles, which he then handed to each of the boys in turn, ostentatiously skipping Terry, who sat shaking his head at the idiocy of his friends, but also secretly feeling a little left out.

Jack, Sipho, Liam and John immediately wolfed their shares, which they washed down with beers, but David sat looking at his portion for quite some time until Liam finally snorted with exasperation, "*Are you going to eat that, mummy's boy, or do you want to donate it to someone else who will?*"

Jack quickly jumped in to defend his twin, smacking Liam over the head, saying, *"Of course he's going to eat it, you prat! Come on, bru, we haven't got all day here."* David, casting a fearful glance at his twin brother, nervously ate the mushrooms. From experience he knew that it didn't do to show his brother up in front of his friends. Then the boys settled around the campfire again, sipping their drinks and chewing the fat somewhat nervously as they waited for something to happen.

After about half-an-hour, Jack grumbled, *"Well, this is a total bomb. I feel nothing at all!"*

"Just wait a bit and see," advised Liam, who, truth be told, was feeling a little worried that the mushrooms were, indeed, a dud.

Just then, David piped up, *"Hey guys, look there! Check it out – inside the fire. Oh. My. God. It's alive... How can that thing possibly be alive in that heat?"* The boys all gazed intently into the fire and were astonished to discover that there was a small, scaly lizard crawling around amongst the coals, seemingly unaffected by the heat of the flames.

"No way... Guys, look, it's growing!" gasped John, as the small lizard began to expand until it was the size of a large dog, its neck extending, as it writhed and swayed in the flames. Then, all around the lizard, smaller reptiles emerged, each undergoing the same transformation, as they expanded until there were ten or more serpentine beings, dancing and writhing around each other in the flames. David jumped up and ran shrieking into the forest, whilst the other four boys sat transfixed, watching the spectacle before them. Terry, who could not see what the others were seeing, was most alarmed when David ran off and so he followed him into the forest to ensure that he would be safe.

The reptiles in the flames began writhing closer and closer together in the middle of the fire and then they combined to form a single, many-headed serpent that transformed, before their very eyes, into a tall, naked green woman with wild, writhing hair. The woman observed the boys with a stern expression on her face; the flames which clothed her body and hair changing in colour from bright orange-red to an iridescent, luminous green. Up to this point, the stories that the boys told all, more-or-less, coincided. But, what happened after the appearance of the woman seems to have differed for each of the boys. Following, are the six individual stories.

Liam's story:
Liam was feeling rather excited at the success of his little treat for his friends and, although his heart was pounding at the sight of the fire lizards and the green woman, he was probably less fearful than his friends as he had already on several occasions consumed hallucinogens with his older cousin, Rex.

The green woman turned to look directly at Liam and her frown deepened as she stepped out of the fire and glided over to him. At this point, Liam did begin to feel extremely fearful and he cowered away from the woman as she towered over him, easily eight feet tall; her eyes glowing with an eerie, green fire.

"Liam, you are a nasty, disrespectful little boy. You think you can eat my children for your own entertainment?" she hissed, somehow speaking without moving her lips, directly into his mind. Liam tried to step away from her and stumbled backwards over a rock, to land sprawled on his backside in front of the terrifying spectacle. *"You are sly and*

untrustworthy because you don't believe that you can trust anyone else. This is the result of your experiences, but the time has come for you to decide to choose differently. Little boy, you are a snake, so slither away and hide until I say you may return!" she spat at the cowering boy. At her words, Liam felt a curious crawling sensation on his skin. Looking down at his bare arm, to his horror he saw scales beginning to cover his skin. And then he felt a strange tingling in his body and his arms and legs began to shrink, eventually to disappear. Within seconds, Liam the boy had disappeared, to be replaced by Liam the mole snake, who instantly slithered away into the bushes, in an attempt to get away from the strange woman. He was to remain there until he eventually fell asleep and awoke the following morning to find himself, once more, in his human form, but covered in scratches and twigs and leaves from sleeping all night in the bushes.

Sipho's story:

Sipho had been feeding his face pretty much constantly the entire time the boys had been sitting around the campfire. He was a large lad, who tended to obesity, and food was both his comfort and his main entertainment. It was only when the woman stepped out of the fire and glided towards him, that the handful of potato crisps was finally arrested in its journey towards his mouth, which remained, however, open and gaping as he observed her progress.

"Sipho, you are a greedy, disrespectful boy," the woman spoke directly into his mind in an icy-cold voice. "Look around you – you have defiled my home with the litter of your gluttony." Sipho looked around himself and saw, to his shame, that the woman was right – he was surrounded by empty wrappers and bags and papers and beer cans. "You eat to fill the vacuum inside of yourself, but it never gets filled up. Only when you learn to love yourself will you ever feel sated. Right now, you are a pig and so you shall remain until i decide that you may return!* she said, with disgust, and, at that, Sipho felt his body begin to change into that of a massive, tusked bushpig, covered in wiry bristles. Sipho the pig began to root around on the outskirts of the fire. He would eventually fall asleep beside the fire until the next morning when he would discover that he had regained his usual form, with his blue jeans split right down the back to expose his ample rump, clad in bright-yellow jocks.

John's story:
John began to giggle nervously when the green woman approached him, silently gliding over the ground. *"John, you think everything is a joke! And yet, littering and despoiling my home and treating others with disrespect is no laughing matter,"* she said with derision, directly into his mind. *"You laugh because you don't want others to see that you have no self-respect. You are just a silly little monkey-boy and that is how you will remain until I say that you may return,"* she said with contempt, turning away as John disappeared, to be replaced by a small grey monkey, which immediately scampered away into the nearest tree, where it sat chattering in fear until the following morning, acutely aware of the presence of leopards and various other predators in the forest. When John awoke the following morning, he was extremely startled to find himself up in a tree and, in his surprise, he over-balanced and fell to the ground, landing somewhat heavily, and very embarrassingly, on his rear end. Somehow, for a change, he didn't feel the need to giggle about

this at all. The resultant bruise was to take over a week to fade.

David's story:

David's well-developed sense of self preservation had ensured that he hadn't run very far into the forest after the fire serpents had appeared and terrified him out of his wits. He dove under a thick clump of bushes and sat there trembling, his eyes closed and his hands over his ears, until he felt someone pull the bushes aside and speak sternly to him, directly into his mind. *"Open your eyes, little boy. It doesn't help to hide, you know. You have to take responsibility for your actions."* David opened his eyes and squinted at the tall, stern, green woman standing there before him.

She wasn't nearly as frightening as the fire serpents and so he lowered his hands and said, *"Who are you?"*

"It doesn't matter who I am; what matters is who you are," she said. *"You are so much more than you ever allow yourself to be, David. But you don't spend any time at all trying to find out who you are. Rather, you choose to keep trying to be what others tell you to be and doing what others tell you to do. You are a mouse, David. You need to find your backbone, little boy, and you are going to remain a tiny little mouse until I decide that you may return."* With that, David felt a tingling on the surface of his skin and, as he watched in horror, coarse grey hair began to sprout all over his body, a long tail began to emerge and he felt himself shrinking, as his hands grew sharp claws. The little grey mouse, David, shrank even further into the bushes, his tiny heart pounding at the thought of all the terrifying predators that were out there in the forest, just waiting to harm him. When he awoke the following morning and discovered that he had regained his

human form, he had never felt more grateful in his entire life. He would never forget the fear and vulnerability that he had experienced as a small mouse and would thereafter always be grateful for his human form, which suddenly felt much safer than he had ever imagined that it could.

Jack's story:

When the green woman approached Jack, there was sadness in her eyes. She spoke directly into his mind, *"Jack, of all the boys, I am the most disappointed in you. The other boys look up to you and yet you fail to provide real leadership, despite all your natural talents and abilities. Look at how you have littered and despoiled my home. Look at the disrespectful way in which you have treated my children. You could have convinced your friends to do better and yet you did nothing but allow this travesty to happen. I had expected better from you than this,"* she said, shaking her head sadly. *"You could have been a lion and yet you did nothing. So now you won't be able to do anything, even if you wanted to! You will remain like this until I say that you may return,"* she said, turning away as Jack felt his body becoming rigid and then, suddenly, he was unable to move at all, his entire body turning to stone. It was only when the first rays of sunlight touched the campsite that he was gradually able to move his stiff body, which had become the perfect perch for hundreds of forest birds, singing the dawn chorus. He would later discover his clothing and hair to be absolutely covered in bird droppings.

Terry's story:

Terry went running after David to ensure that he was safe, grabbing his torch out of his jacket pocket to light his way. Unbeknownst to him, in his concern for the other boy, he had run at top speed right past the thicket of bushes in which David was cowering and onto a narrow path through the forest. After scrambling down the path in the ever-decreasing light for another ten minutes, calling David's name, he realized that he should slow down. Common sense told him that he had probably run right past David and also that it was dangerous to stumble into the forest at night on an unknown path. Noticing that there was a clearing straight ahead, he walked a few paces forward so as to catch his breath and to take stock before heading back to the campsite.

Terry was about to turn back when he noticed a strange green glow beneath a massive Yellowwood tree that was festooned with old man's beard. He stepped closer, his curiosity getting the better of him and then he felt his jaw drop open in surprise as the green light resolved into a beautiful, green woman, whose long, twig-and-leaf bedecked, dark-green hair was draped for modesty around her otherwise naked body.

"*What... who... who are you?*" Terry stammered, wondering whether this was the famed Green Lady whom his father had told him about when he was just a little boy.

"*I'm the spirit of the forest,*" she smilingly replied, "*But I'm really more interested in who you are. Or rather, in who you think you are!*"

"*I'm... I'm not sure I follow,*" said Terry tentatively, thinking that this was probably the strangest conversation he had ever had and wondering whether the other boys had found a way of putting some of the mushrooms into his food.

"*Well, let's work through it, then, shall we?*" she asked, sitting down on a fallen log and patting the seat beside her to indicate that Terry should sit down too, which he, rather hesitantly, did. As he did so, he experienced the strangest sensation of expansion; as if he was growing and becoming something or someone more than who he currently was. It was a wonderfully warm and deeply profound experience.

"Terry, are you your body?" she asked.

"Well... no, I have a body but I'm pretty sure that I'm more than just this meat-suit I'm currently living in," said Terry, finding this conversation increasingly strange.

"Correct answer. So, are you your thoughts?" she asked.

"No, because I can stop thinking for a moment or two and I still continue existing," said Terry, starting to enjoy the dialogue.

"OK, are you your possessions?"

"Oh, definitely not – I can lose all that I have and I will still be me, although I'd be pretty pissed off to lose my computer! But then, I'd still just be me, but an angrier version of me. And, when the anger finally passed, I'd still just be me, so I guess I'm also not my emotions or even my experiences or my memories of past experiences," said Terry, who had had similar discussions with his father in the past.

"Right, so then Terry, tell me who you really are," she asked, smiling gently at him.

"Well, I'm, I suppose, kinda the observer of my life. Something... unchanged and unchanging that is always there watching the play of my life, but not really getting involved," replied Terry, reaching for the truth deep within himself.

"Well, Terry, I suppose that, in a similar way, I am the watcher, the observer of the forest; of all Forest wherever it may be," the Lady said. *"Just like your life, Terry's life, is an expression of a higher being, so the forest is an expression of me.*

But tell me, Terry, why do you think you are here in this reality? What do you think is the purpose of your life; what is the purpose of Terry's life?"

"Wow, that's a really difficult question," said Terry. "I'm not sure of that yet. I mean, some people seem to know that their purpose is to be a doctor or a fireman and to save lives or something. But I don't yet know what I want to do with my life."

"Terry, don't confuse purpose with the roles that we play. Doctor or fireman is merely a role that we can choose to play in this game of life. It is not our purpose, although many people make the mistake of thinking that their career is their purpose and then they feel cheated when they don't feel fulfilled in the way they had thought they would. People change and their roles, duties and responsibilities change, but their overall purpose never, ever changes."

"OK, so then what IS the purpose of our lives?" asked Terry.

"There is only ever one purpose to any life and that is to express your most authentic self in each moment," said the Lady.

"Really?" asked Terry, feeling more than just a little confused.

"Yes," said the Lady, smiling again. "But the trick is that you have to really reach deep to find and connect with your most authentic self in each moment. And so we return to my original question. Who are you, Terry? Are you the small, limited, human boy that you currently experience yourself to be, or are you the expanded, most magnificent version of yourself that you can possibly find in each moment? It's a perspective issue, Terry, and it's your choice as to which *perspective you will choose to take. And so, Terry, who are you going to choose to be... right now?"*

And, with these words, the Lady faded away, leaving Terry with a multitude of questions dancing around in his mind. He returned to the campsite where he found the other boys fast asleep around the fire and so he too got into his sleeping bag and gradually fell asleep.

The following morning the other boys were strangely subdued and refused to discuss their experiences of the previous night. But Terry was relieved to see that they were all seemingly unharmed, apart from some dirt, scratches, bruises and torn clothing. He knew that they had had a very lucky escape and he decided that he would never again go camping with this lot of idiots. Besides, his mind was buzzing with so many ideas that he found himself quite uninterested in normal adolescent discussions.

In time, once the boys returned to their normal lives, they gradually began to talk about, and to share, their experiences in the forest that night.

One thing was certain, though; the experience had irrevocably changed each of the boys for life, and mostly for the good.

CHAPTER 9
WRITING HER INTO THE STORY

During my six months in Knysna, I spent a considerable amount of time in its modest, but surprisingly well-stocked library, doing research on the place, its history and its people. At the front of the library there was a small, but prominent, display of books written by local authors, only one of which was instantly recognisable. *The Amazon Code* was a high-class, action-packed thriller, about a group of scientists who had discovered a secret code, written into the X-chromosome that, once activated, facilitated the breeding of a super-race of female warriors. The luminous-green DNA double helix glowing against a stark black background with the title picked out in large, gold-embossed capital letters proclaimed its status as a bestseller. The book, that had been written by South African author, Steven Small, had won two prestigious debut novel awards, had spent two weeks on the New York Times bestseller list and had enjoyed an intense spate of international popularity a couple of years earlier. It was still on the bestseller lists of most bookstores, albeit considerably further down the list than when it had first appeared on the bookshelves. The Librarian at the Knysna library breathlessly confided in me that the author, who had grown up in Knysna, was temporarily renting a holiday cottage just outside of town for peace and privacy so as to facilitate the process of writing his next book. He had personally signed the Library's copy of

The Amazon Code, she whispered, clearly still completely star struck.

I wasted no further time thinking about Steven Small, as I was absolutely certain that an author of his stature would never be interested in contributing to the work of an unpublished, would-be debut author such as myself. But, as fate would have it, two months later I met the man himself as I was enjoying a beer at Harry B's, a popular Knysna pub, on a Friday evening. It was actually my second beer that I was nursing as I waited for the young lady who was to have been my date for the evening to arrive. She was over thirty minutes late and was not responding to my text messages. I had just decided to write off the evening and to pick up a burger-to-go and some videos for a lonely night in, when a tall, stout man with a full red beard and a commanding presence threw open the door to the pub. He hesitated on the doorstep for a moment, as it waiting for his presence to be noticed, and then he swaggered in, checking the responses of the patrons seated at the small tables on the way to the bar. He had the air of one who was used to being recognized and who thoroughly enjoyed the attention. The man ordered his double whisky-on-the-rocks and threw the banknote at the barman, flamboyantly exhorting him to, *"keep the change,"* and only then did he deign to notice me sitting right there beside him.

"Quiet for a Friday night, hey?" he spoke in a deep, booming voice, his restless eyes roving the premises as if seeking out someone more important than I. Mildly amused at the man's arrogance, and apparently having nothing better lined up for the evening, I decided to satisfy my curiosity as to his identity.

"You look familiar. Have I met you before?" I asked, deliberately pandering to his ego, but also telling the truth.

The man did look slightly familiar to me in the manner of a celebrity, whose picture you have often seen, but have never met in person.

It seemed as if those were the magic words required to unlock my companion's attention, as he swivelled around in his seat to face me for the first time, holding out his right hand to introduce himself, *"Steven Small, by name, but certainly not by stature! I'm the author of the New York Times bestseller,* The Amazon Code. *Currently residing here in Knysna and writing my second novel."* I immediately realised that my expected role for the evening would be that of admirer, paying obeisance to The Great Author. But I decided to voluntarily play that role anyway as I secretly hoped that there might just possibly be some benefit to myself in spending time with a bestselling author.

"Wow!" I enthused. *"Who would have thought that I would meet a bestselling author on a Friday night in sleepy, little Knysna! So, how's it going? Your second novel, I mean?"* My companion, who had been visibly preening at the first part of my response, began to scowl and lost some of his bravado at the second part. Clearly the writing was not proceeding as anticipated. I didn't enquire any further about his current book, but ordered another beer and proceeded to pepper him with questions about his experiences with his first book that were designed to stroke his ego. By the time that he was downing his third double whisky, the first two having disappeared rather alarmingly rapidly, it seemed as if I had gained his trust, as the man's confident mask had begun somewhat to slip. Steven admitted to me that things weren't going that well with the book. Having made that admission appeared to unlock the real person inside of the larger-than-

life persona and Steven proceeded to reveal to me a tale of woe, very familiar to the authors of successful books.

The writing of his first book had been so easy, he confided. It had just flowed directly from his mind onto the paper; almost as if he were taking dictation rather than actually creating the work. Although he had personally thought that the book showed some promise, he had never expected it to do as well as it had, particularly once the rejection slips began to flow back from publishers to whom he had sent the manuscript. *"I thought: oh well, at least I've still got my day job, it's not like I need this book to sell in order to be OK. It would be money for jam if it did, though,"* he confided in me. It turned out that Steven had been teaching English at a small community college before his book was published and I thought to myself that he had probably needed the cash back then far more than he was now willing to let on.

But then, the miraculous occurred. It was the kind of story that inspires would-be authors to keep going, against all odds. A young assistant-to-the-editor of a small, but promising new publishing house that specialized in thrillers, seeking to make her mark in the competitive world of publishing, picked up Steven's book from the slush pile to read during her summer vacation. When she returned to work a week later, she was gushing so profusely about the book, that the senior editor, who had his eye on the young woman, in more ways than one, agreed to take a look at the work. Well, it turned out that the editor agreed with his young protégé and, before too long, Steven found himself polishing his novel with the assistance of a competent editor; a modest advance alleviating some of the financial pressure that he had been under since his divorce had been finalized a year earlier.

Steven's book, when it was released, vastly exceeded all expectations and made the career of the lovely young assistant editor, as well as the fortunes of the small publishing house. The two awards that Steven garnered considerably boosted his sales and when the book landed on the New York Times bestseller list, his future as an author seemed assured.

The proceeds from book sales were sufficient to allow Steven to quit his dead-end job and to focus on the far more prestigious and, to him, fulfilling job of being a bestselling author. I could see that he had absolutely relished the attention and the accolades. It was clear to me that the book signings and readings, the award ceremonies and the book tours all offered the perfect boost to Steven's burgeoning ego. He took to wearing crew neck sweaters, a goatee and small, wire-rimmed glasses that, I suspect, he believed conveyed upon himself an authorial air. He absolutely relished the awestruck fawning that he began to consider his due. He particularly relished the attentions of young ladies of a literary bent who were flatteringly eager to bed a bestselling author.

For a while it was simply wonderful but, of course, on one book alone is rarely an author's reputation based and so, after a year or two, the pressure to produce another bestseller began mounting. The small publishing house that had initially optioned Steven's book had subsequently been acquired by a massive, well-known publishing house, due, largely, to the success of Steven's first book. Steven's newly appointed agent was what he privately termed, *"a real ball-buster,"* who increasingly turned up the pressure for an encore to Steven's debut success. He was given a generous six-figure advance on his next book, the first full draft of which was due in just under a year. But Steven was simply unable to produce the goods. When he sat down to write he found himself to be completely blocked. He spent hours developing wild plot lines on a series of brightly-coloured post-it notes stuck to a blank wall in his home. But, when he tried to write them in book form, they just didn't work. His characters were not believable, his dialogue was clunky and his plots boring and predictable. Steven's agent began phoning him almost daily for progress reports. Steven was in serious trouble, particularly since his advance had long since been absorbed into the increasingly luxuriant lifestyle which he had considered to be his due as the famous author of a New York Times bestseller. In short, Steven was in deep trouble.

In desperation, he decided to return to his childhood hometown and rent a modest cottage in a quiet, remote place outside of town, away from all distractions. But, by the time I met him, he had already squandered three months and was nowhere nearer to completing the work that was expected of him. *"To tell you the truth,"* he sadly confided in me, somewhat slurring his words due to the volume of whisky he had consumed, *"I came here tonight to get plastered 'cause I know it's over. I can't do it. I know that now. I'm a big, fat failure!"* He lowered his head onto his folded arms on the bar counter and began, very loudly, to sob.

Thoroughly alarmed at this turn of events, I clumsily patted his shoulder, the masculine equivalent of a comforting hug, as I glanced around me, shrugging in embarrassment at the smirks and questioning glances. When the sobs showed no sign of abating, I realized that I would have to take some action to salvage at least some portion of my reputation in this small town. So I put my arm around Steven's shoulder and heaved him to his feet, throwing a couple of bills onto the counter to cover the cost of our drinks and half-carried, half-dragged him to the door and into my car, which was conveniently parked just outside the pub. I took him back to my apartment, where I dumped him onto the couch, removed his shoes and covered him with a blanket. This was definitely not the way I had anticipated spending my Friday evening when I had so hopefully changed into my only clean shirt a few hours earlier!

The following morning, Steven was shamefaced and subdued as he accepted the large mug of freshly brewed coffee I handed him. This pale, quiet, diminished man was a very far cry from the bombastic egotist of the previous night and I fancy that he regretted sharing with me the many confidences of the night before. After Steven had tidied himself up a bit, I drove him back to his own car. Winding down his window he mumbled, face averted, "Sorry, man, for falling apart like that. You were a good friend. Thank you." And then he put on a pair of dark glasses to hide his hangover from the cheery early morning light and slowly drove away.

I thought of Steven a few times in the following weeks but did not expect to hear from him again as I knew that someone with such an over-developed ego would probably have deeply regretted showing such weakness to a stranger. So, consequently, I was greatly surprised to encounter Steven whilst jogging on a deserted beach very early one morning about four weeks later. I hardly recognized him at first, as he had lost so much weight. He had also lost both the swaggering braggadocio and the hangdog self-pity I had previously witnessed in the pub and in my apartment, almost a month earlier. This new, streamlined, Steven was clad in a sweat-drenched tracksuit and sported a clear complexion and bright, hope-filled eyes. He looked, in a word, healthy.

I'm not sure that I would have acknowledged Steven, due to the less than felicitous circumstances of our last meeting, but, as it turned out, he recognized me, saying, *"Peter, hey, it's you! How are you? How strange that I should bump into you here. I've been thinking about you a lot lately and I've been planning to give you a call!"* Well, that certainly surprised me! Steven fell into an easy, relaxed jog, matching me pace-for-pace and, when I realized that there would be no escaping this interaction, I suggested that we grab a cup of coffee together at a beachfront coffee shop a few hundred meters away, which is exactly what we did.

"Peter, I've been told to share my story with you, for inclusion in your book," were his first astonishing words to me upon sitting down with our coffees. That surprised me greatly, particularly since I had not told Steven that I was writing a book.

"Really? Who told you that?" I enquired.

Steven regarded me with a quizzical smile and said, *"Just listen to my story and then you can decide if you want to include it in your book or not."* It turned out that Steven's persona that I had encountered in the pub had concealed a high-octane secret! And, for some reason, I had been selected to be the means of revealing this secret. My heart pounded with ever-increasing excitement as Steven's story unfolded.

Steven had never dreamt of being a bestselling author. In fact, he had never dreamed of anything much at all. Steven, despite the best efforts of his over-achieving parents and the teachers in the top schools to which he was sent, was the classic under-achiever. And proud of it. He simply couldn't be bothered to take the effort to excel at anything much at school. And, though his ill-deserved final year marks (and the influence and legacy of his over-achieving father and grandfather) allowed him to scrape into a good university, he had absolutely no idea of what he wanted to do with his life once there. He knew that he really loved beautiful girls and that he liked beer and having a good time with his friends. But he couldn't be bothered putting effort into anything other than these activities. It all seemed rather futile and a bit too much like hard work. He decided to study English; his reasoning being that he could already speak the language and so it would probably not require too much effort on his part! Steven's undistinguished university career was spent indulging in all his favourite activities and doing the minimum work required to scrape through his courses.

Steven's room mate, Darrell, was his polar opposite, being a quiet, intense, studious and socially inept pre-med student. Darrell spent every spare moment he had working on his manuscript, as he fancied himself as an author and was only in medical school due to the ambitions and sacrifice of his father, who was his only surviving relative. Toward the end of Steven's third and final year at university, he entered the dorm room to pick up a jacket on his way out to a pub with a bunch of his friends. He was surprised to encounter Darrell in a state of feverish excitement.

"It's finished, man! My book, I finished it today!" he crowed, before Steven could enquire as to why he was so agitated. *"And, I want you to be the first to read it. Nobody else even knows that I've been writing a book! You're studying English and so you can read it and tell me what you think. It might need a bit of editing and stuff, but you must be absolutely honest with me,"* the words gushed from Darrell's mouth. Well, Steven himself wasn't overly excited to be

accorded the honour, but he had grown fond of Darrell over the three years of their co-habitation and he felt sorry for the guy due to his lack of friends.

So he said, *"Sure, man. I'll read it when I have a moment,"* and he tossed the manuscript onto the chaotic pile of papers on his desk.

Later that night when Steven returned to the dorm, Darrell wasn't there, which was extremely unusual for his anti-social room mate. But Steven thought that Darrell had probably gone out to celebrate finishing his manuscript and could possibly, against all odds, have gotten lucky. And so he went to bed without thinking any further about it. However, the following morning, Steven heard the shocking news that Darrell and his father had been killed in a car accident with a drunken student, who had walked away from the accident absolutely unscathed, the previous night. Steven never did read Darrell's manuscript at that time and it landed up in a box of papers and files when he packed up his dorm room a few months later, in possession of a degree in English, obtained by the skin of his teeth. He landed an uninspiring job teaching English at the community college where he met his future wife, Mary. Two years later they were married and Steven's boxes of university papers landed up at the back of a cupboard in their modest apartment, where they were to remain until Steven and Mary were divorced twelve years later.

It was when Steven was sorting through all his old boxes and papers so as to decide what to take with him to his new, smaller bachelor pad that he rediscovered his old university room mate's unread manuscript. In a bout of nostalgia for his earlier life, he sat down and began paging through the manuscript. Five hours of solid reading later, he finally looked up from the manuscript in astonishment. The writing was execrable, the characters wooden and unbelievable, the dialogue clunky in the extreme. But the plot line was absolutely brilliant! It caught Steven's imagination in a way that very few books had done in the past and the germ of an idea began to rapidly develop in Steven's mind. He could re-write this book and turn it into something really great. He felt unbelievably inspired and energized in a way that he had never before experienced. He would write the book that Darrell had not been able to! It would be the perfect distraction from the misery of living alone again for the first time in twelve years. And then he would attempt to have the book published as a tribute to poor Darrell's tragically short and unfulfilled life. And that was exactly what he did. Except for one minor detail. Steven put his own name on the manuscript.

In writing the book, Steven had never before felt such enthusiasm or experienced such boundless energy. He could barely contain his impatience throughout his boring work day at the college and could hardly wait for the moment when he could return home at night and start on his real work. He worked through most of every night and more-or-less sleep-walked his way through each day. He took every last day of leave that he could spare and as many sick days as he felt he could get away with. Holidays and weekends were spent feverishly writing. He was completely in thrall to his muse and he had never before felt so alive and purpose-filled. Within a year the book was complete and within another six months Steven had been signed by the publishing house. Another year later he was able to leave his job, without a single backward glance, and devote himself to being an author.

There were moments when he felt guilty about stealing Darrell's ideas and plot line for his own novel, but he justified this by telling himself that Darrell was dead and had had no other family who could have inherited his work. And besides, the book that Steven had written was all his own work... and it was brilliant! Darrell's book had been dreadful and would never have been published. The manuscript would simply have languished in a drawer somewhere. At least this way it gained a life of its own, which Darrell would never, in a million years, have been able to give it.

"But, I guess that on some level I always felt bad that I had benefited so much from poor Darrell's misfortune," admitted Steven. *"In some locked room within my heart was deep regret for what I had done. What I recently realized was that this was what had been blocking me as a writer. Which brings us to the events of that morning, four weeks ago, when I drove away from you, standing outside the pub."*

Steven had arrived back at his rental cottage feeling like death warmed over. In addition to the misery that was his life at that moment, he was also severely hung-over. He really had no clue as to what he should do next. After a shower and a couple of aspirin, he threw himself down onto a deckchair outside and morosely gazed, unaffected, at the beauty of the forest around him.

He must have been sleeping for some time because, when a sound awoke him, the sun had already begun to set. He opened his eyes to discover, to his absolute shock and amazement, that he wasn't alone. Sitting in the other deckchair, backlit by a sky afire with brilliant streaks of cerise, burnt amber and gold was a strange-looking, green woman who winked at him as his mouth fell open in shock.

"At last! I've been waiting to speak to you," she smiled as she spoke, without moving her lips, directly into his mind. *"I'm just a dream, so don't worry about it. Just be quiet*

and listen to what I have to say," she reassured him. Steven found himself relaxing at her words and he leaned forward to better hear what she next had to say.

"Steven, you know that you are blocked by your guilt and shame over what you did. You are going to have to come clean about it because otherwise you will never reach your full potential as an author, which is vastly beyond what you can currently envisage. Your first book is nothing in comparison to what you will write in future."

"But, if I tell my agent and publisher about what I did, they will demand that I repay my advance and they will never publish anything else that I might write," Steven objected.

"They will publish your next book because it's going to be brilliant and you will admit what you have done after the second book is published. Your reputation as an author will be established and they will never drop their cash-cow. Pay attention now, Steven. Peter Allen is the means by which you are going to tell your public about what you have done."

"Peter Allen? But... what has he got to do with it?" asked Steven in some confusion.

"Peter is writing his own book, which you would know if you had been paying attention to anything else, other than your own ego," she remarked, "Peter Allen is going to include your story in his book and you are going to give him all the assistance he requires to accomplish that. Your new book will be published long before his, as you already have an agent and publisher lined up and he is going to have to find his own way towards publishing his book."

This was all very unexpected, but Steven had other concerns, "But, I'm completely blocked," he objected. "I've been trying to write this book for months now and it's going absolutely nowhere!"

"*The book will be a best-seller because I'm going to tell you what to write. Now, stop feeling sorry yourself and get in front of your typewriter and listen to your heart, which is where you will hear my voice in future.*"

Steven stared at the woman in astonishment, as a tiny flicker of hope ignited deep within his heart. "*But... why would you help me?*" he asked.

"*Because I need something from you,*" she answered. "*I have my own story that I need to tell, and this story will be highlighted in your book, which will be a massive bestseller and will provide me with the largest possible audience for my message. Steven, I need you to write me into the story!*"

"*Well, fine,*" Steven replied, still unsure about all of this, "*But I can't see people wanting to read a book featuring a Green Lady. Albeit a very beautiful one,*" he hastened to add as he saw her frown appear.

"*You idiot! Obviously you won't be writing about me in the form in which I now appear to you! Your book will highlight the plight of forests all over the world. Now, get going, there is very little time left and much to accomplish!*" she admonished.

"*Wow, that is a simply incredible story!*" I enthused, thrilled to hear that the Green Lady was aware of me and my book, "*And how is the book progressing?*"

"*It's simply brilliant!*" he claimed, with a touch of his old arrogance. "*It's definitely going to be a bestseller, I can just feel it. And it certainly highlights many issues of concern to my lovely green muse.*" More than that, he would not say and so I would simply have to wait, along with everyone else, for his new novel to hit the shelves within the following year. But, for the first time, I began to feel some real confidence in my own work and its possibility of being published. After all, if my book was to be the means by which Steven's story would be told to his public, then surely my book too would eventually see the light of day?

But I realised that, as exciting as it would be to have my own book published, it would pale in comparison to the privilege of actually encountering the lovely Green Lady myself.

Chapter 10
The Water of Life

I met Sarah at the weekly Farmers' Market where she had a stall selling her home-grown organic vegetables and cut flowers. A small, hand-painted sign informed me that she also offered her services as a dowser for water. To me she represented the quintessential "hippy-chick" with her filthy feet bare, despite the cold, her eclectic layers of colourful clothing and her wild, long hair sporting several tiny plaits, threaded through with wild flowers, bright ribbons and feathers. She exuded a vivid energy, abundant vitality and an aura of irrepressible joy.

I found it impossible not to engage her in conversation. *"Wow, you certainly are an excellent advertisement for the benefits of your products,"* I remarked, *"I have rarely encountered anyone so disgustingly healthy-looking!"*

"Yes, it's true, I am blessed with a lot of energy and very good health," she effused, *"But it certainly wasn't always the case. Just two years ago I was a completely different person."*

"How so?" I enquired, sensing the possibility of an interesting story.

"Well, I'm due for a break anyway," she said, as she winked at her co-worker, *"How about you buy me a veggie juice in exchange for a story?"* Well, how could I possibly refuse such an enticing offer, especially one made by so charming a young lady! Minutes later we were comfortably

ensconced on a couple of logs under the shade of a massive, overhanging oak tree; me nursing a steaming mug of cappuccino and her sipping at a paper cup of disgusting-looking, green goop. This, then, is Sarah's story.

Sarah's parents had both been in their forties when Sarah was born and it was clear from the start that she would always be an only child. Sarah's father was a Professor of mathematics and her mother the Chief Librarian in the university medical library and consequently Sarah grew up in a quiet, subdued and bookish environment in which she was related to as a small adult and encouraged to engage in indoor pursuits such as reading, chess and research, rather than sport or social activities. As a result, she grew up rather quiet and shy and, although she was academically and intellectually advanced, her social skills were sadly underdeveloped.

Upon leaving school, Sarah decided to study accounting at university, a decision of which her parents wholeheartedly approved, viewing it as a dignified and respectable career which would provide their daughter with ample means of supporting herself. As a day student at the university for which her parents worked and, electing to stay at home in order to save money, Sarah chose not to participate in the varied social activities on offer to a first-year student. She experienced her fellow students to be incomprehensibly infantile and their company puerile at best. Sarah vastly preferred to spend her time studying, reading or taking solitary walks or runs in the park. Sometimes, though, in the quiet privacy of her own heart, she did experience a small, wistful pang of yearning and regret when she observed other students laughing and horsing around. And, every now and then, on yet another Saturday evening spent playing chess with her father or reading aloud to her mother from some worthy tome, she would feel just the smallest stab of dissatisfaction, loneliness and a desire for something, well... more.

One crisp autumn morning, as Sarah sprinted up the final incline in her regular circuit around the lake, she noticed a young man with rather attractive legs ahead of her and, giving way to her well-developed competitive streak, Sarah picked up her pace and steamed up the hill to reach the top ahead of the young man, thereby inadvertently providing him with a glorious view of her own shapely legs, outlined in form-fitting yoga pants, as she did so. At the top of the hill, Sarah focused on performing her usual series of stretches which, had she but been aware of the fact, were perfectly designed to showcase her supple and slender young body to its very best advantage.

"In training, are you?" a smooth, masculine voice interrupted her reverie, causing Sarah to start and yelp with surprise, whipping around to find herself staring into the most meltingly gorgeous, deepest-chocolate-brown eyes she had ever encountered.

"Training? What? Oh, no, um... it's just my time to um... think and prepare for my studies," she responded, mentally kicking herself for her verbal clumsiness, but noticing as she did so the way his dark hair curled so enticingly around his gorgeous ears and the dimple that appeared in his left cheek as he smiled at her and... Sarah was instantly, irrevocably and disastrously smitten! Nothing in her quiet and modest eighteen years of life had prepared her for the beauty, for what she considered to be, the sheer perfection of this magnificent man.

What followed was, from Sarah's rather naive viewpoint, the romance of a lifetime. She surrendered herself, body, mind and soul to Matt, and he became the focal point and the centre of her life. She neglected her studies so as to spend every moment accommodating herself to Matt's whims and fitting in with his rather erratic schedule of class attendance. She would lie awake for hours just watching him sleep, quietly sighing at the pleasure of being able to study his gorgeous face for as long as she pleased without him being aware of it. But alas, as Sarah was shortly to discover, Matt was not quite as committed to her as she was to him.

What followed was a story as old as time, but for Sarah, the betrayal and loss of her first real love were completely devastating. When she inadvertently walked in on Matt and Lily, a pretty and popular second-year student, "doing the dirty" in Matt's dorm room, she felt as if she had been dealt a sharp punch to the solar plexus and, even months later, would still feel as if she were unable to breathe properly. Like a wounded animal, Sarah bolted straight home from Matt's dorm room and closeted herself in her room for two weeks. Two weeks in which her parents were unable to console her or even really connect with their daughter at all. Two weeks in which she hardly ate or bathed and remained in her bed with the covers over her head, emerging only intermittently to play Matt's favourite music and bawl her eyes out in a little wet heap on the couch before returning, once more, to bed.

The girl who finally emerged from that room and resumed her studies bore very little resemblance to the Sarah of old. Pale and extremely thin, the light had left her eyes and she was subsequently very rarely seen to smile. There was something dried-out and insubstantial about her, as if all of her life essence, joy and vitality had been wrung out of her. She appeared to be in danger of drifting away on the lightest of breezes. She gave up running in the park and used some of her savings to purchase a treadmill, upon which she exercised every morning. It simply felt safer to be at home than out in the world. Sarah stopped socialising altogether, dividing her time between her classes, the library and her parents' home and single-mindedly threw herself into her studies. As a result, she graduated top of her class three years later, which enabled her to secure an entry-level position in a top firm of chartered accountants, which undertook to pay for Sarah's post-graduate studies and offered her in-service training.

Hard work, native intelligence and dedication to the interests of the business fast-tracked Sarah's career and at the age of thirty-five she was called into a board meeting, at which she was offered a partnership in the firm. As Sarah stood up to leave the boardroom, the principle partner laid a hand upon her shoulder and said, "*Sarah, as a partner you will need to provide leadership and direction to the more junior members of staff and you will also be required to attend various social and networking events. We cannot fault your work ethic, your intelligence and skills, or your dedication to the firm, but you need to work on your people skills and you also need to spend some time socialising with the team. The Board would strongly recommend that you join in some of the work sporting activities and teams in order to start building relationships with your colleagues outside of working hours. I know that you're a keen runner, so how about you joining the running team and then, the hiking club might be a good idea too.*" Of course, Sarah was aware that she hadn't spent any time getting to know her colleagues outside of the work environment, as she was completely disinclined towards social interaction. But she really wanted that partnership and equally really wanted to be favourably viewed by her colleagues and so she agreed to join both the hiking club and the running team.

And so it was that Sarah found herself on a five-day hike in the Knysna forests with a group of her work colleagues during the following December work break. On the second day of the hike Sarah had an experience that would dramatically alter the course of her life.

The team had been hiking since dawn, the trail alternately leading them along isolated pebbly beaches or upwards into dense coastal forest, but always following the breathtaking coastline to their final destination, three days hence. Toward late afternoon, tired and thirsty, their weary muscles aching for a respite, the hikers happened upon an exquisite freshwater pool in the higher forest, surrounded by massive tree ferns, water trickling down from a rocky, moss-covered ledge a few metres above. After consultation of their maps, they realised, with considerable gratitude, that their rest camp for the night was now only two kilometres away. The rest of the party elected to push on to the camp, with the intention of returning to the pool once they had dropped off their backpacks and rested a while. Sarah, however, decided to stay there to bathe her weary body before embarking upon the final two kilometre stretch to the camp. Although she had enjoyed the physical challenge of the hike and the beauty of the forests, she had been finding the first two days of the hike a bit of a strain, as there appeared to be no respite from the constant chatter and intrusion of her colleagues upon her private thoughts. She simply wasn't accustomed to spending so much time with other people and she relished the thought of an uninterrupted hour or two of solitude and the opportunity for silent contemplation of the magnificent natural beauty she had witnessed thus far on the trail.

Once her companions had left and, knowing that they had been the final group on the hike and that she would not be disturbed by any unwelcome intruders, Sarah quickly stripped off all her sweaty clothing and plunged into the icy-cold, crystal clear, sun-dappled water. As she twisted and tumbled, quenching her thirst by simply submerging her mouth in the water, Sarah felt the weariness of the day's hike leaving her body and a delightful feeling of peace and serenity settled over her. She allowed her mind to drift as her body floated in the water, feeling the warmth of the late-afternoon sun on her face and idly listening to the melodic calls of the birds in the trees above.

Gradually she became aware that the water beneath her was heating up, and tiny eddies, as well as stronger currents of warmer water began subtly massaging the aches and pains out of her tired arms, legs and back. Sarah sighed with bliss without giving much thought to what was happening, other than entertaining a vague idea that perhaps parts of the pool had been heated by the sun earlier in the day. Then a series of bubble streams started to tickle her body, which rapidly focused Sarah's mind on her surroundings. Opening her eyes, Sarah noticed that the air had taken on a magnificent liquid golden hue with sparkling dust motes dancing in the beams of light upon the water.

Just a few metres away, a sudden flash of bright blue light sparked above the surface of the water and then disappeared again into the pool. At the same moment Sarah realised that she no longer had to paddle to keep herself afloat in the water – she was being held by a soft, warm embrace of water! Her mind struggling to come up with logical explanations for this phenomenon, Sarah tried to swim back to the edge of the pool, only to discover that her arms and legs were unable to move, but gently swayed back-and-forth in the warm currents of water. She struggled for a moment or two in panic before a soft susurration in her ears gently and inexplicably calmed her down. Although no recognisable words were actually spoken, she understood the meaning: *"Don't be afraid, you're completely safe. Just relax and enjoy."* Sarah felt a deep sense of well-being flood her body and then the little bubbles began caressing her skin again, sending corresponding shivers of delight through her body and mind.

Again she heard the sound in her ears, *"Did you know that most of your own body is composed of water? We are more alike than you realise!"* Now, as the water currents continued to gently massage and relax her body, she felt an answering call from deep within her own being. Gradually, awareness dawned that the water molecules in her own body were answering the call of the watery creature, which had her enthralled. The water within the cells of her body were responding to the siren call of the water molecules in the pool and were gradually awakening and rehydrating and plumping up with energy and life. Although Sarah's mind informed her that it was impossible, she felt the water surrounding her begin seeping into her body, gradually restoring her lifeless, dried-out being to abundant lushness of life for the first time in years. She felt a surge of power and vitality and then vivid images of magnificent natural beauty began to fill her mind. The images grew ever more real, combining with the increasingly powerful bodily sensations in transporting her to an unimaginable realm of majesty and wonder.

She experienced the indescribable thrill of being the mighty waves crashing upon the shoreline. She felt the ecstatic wonder of transitioning from water to vapour and creating massive cloud banks that released deluges of water upon the thirsty Earth. She experienced the mystery of being absorbed by plants and being incorporated into plant tissues, only to be consumed by animals and then humans and then being re-released into the soil upon the death and dissolution of fleshly bodies. Then, all the images coalesced and she became the entire, magnificent, ecstatic water cycle all at once and she realised that she was indeed both a part of the whole and also the whole at the very same time and she whooped with pleasure and howled with joy at the ecstasy and the wonder and the mystery and the miracle of it all.

After what seemed like eons of time, Sarah gradually became aware that the water was cooling and that she needed once more to paddle to keep herself afloat. At the same moment, she heard voices in the distance and she hastened to the edge of the pool to rapidly dry off and dress herself. She had no desire to try and make normal conversation with her companions, so she slipped away into the forest before they re-appeared at the pool. There was no explaining what had happened to her but she knew that some deep thirst within her had been quenched for the very first time in her life.

Enthralled at the story that Sarah had just related to me, I asked her whether she had any theories as what had actually happened to her that day in the pool. *"My being was rehydrated,"* she said, *"I was re-infused with life and joy and pleasure and I was reminded of my connection to all that is. I realised that I wasn't alone at all; I was a part of something much bigger. It gave me a sense of meaning and purpose in my life and somehow the hurt that I had been carrying for all those years was dissolved and carried away by the water. I realised that I needed to live my life, rather than simply existing and so I made a few changes!"*

It transpired that the latter was a monumental understatement! Upon returning to the city at the end of her vacation, Sarah relinquished her precious partnership, resigned her job and liquidated all of her considerable assets. Within a few months, she moved to Knysna where she purchased a smallholding in an eco village and began growing organic vegetables and indigenous flowers. She also discovered that she had an uncanny talent for finding water on any property and so she began to offer her dowsing services to property developers and home owners. Somehow her experience with the water spirit had increased her sensitivity to the presence of water. This was to become her main means of supporting herself.

"But, Sarah, who or what do you think you encountered in that pool in the forest? Do you have any theories?" I asked, feeling somehow dissatisfied with the abrupt ending to the story.

"I don't suppose I'll ever know for sure; perhaps some kind of elemental water spirit or perhaps even the spirit of the forest itself," said Sarah, smiling and shrugging her shoulders. *"But somehow it allowed me to find my connection to the flow of life, to the rhythms of the forest and to myself, most of all. I'm certain that my supernatural experience in the water is what has allowed me to become such a successful water dowser – I'm able to connect with the water of life, wherever it*

may be found. I'm rejuvenated, revitalised and rehydrated. And life is so good!"

Well, this was very clear just from looking at Sarah and, as I left her that day, I wondered if I had time to pay the forest pool a quick visit myself...

CHAPTER 11
FOREST FUN & GAMES

I first met Geoffrey propping up the bar at a popular local watering hole called Harry B's, his entire body loudly proclaiming his utter dejection for all to behold. He was hunched over, staring into his drink with dark-ringed eyes, a greenish, waxy pallor adorning his youngish, once handsome, but now, sadly, rather jowly face. Normally I avoid drunks like the plague and miserable drunks even more so, but something in the way that Geoffrey systematically shredded his beer mat and lobbed the pieces one-by-one into an empty beer glass on the counter in front of him suggested to my journalistic instincts the whiff of a story just desperate to be told. Seeing as I myself was feeling a little lonely and at a bit of a loss on that particular evening, I sat down on the bar stool next to Geoffrey, plonked my beer down on the counter in front of me and introduced myself.

An hour would pass before I would awaken to the fact that my beer was warm and flat, my nether regions were numb and I had pins-and-needles in my left leg. Somehow I had serendipitously stumbled upon the mother lode-an absolute doozy of a story that revealed another, totally unexpected, side to the Green Lady! Well, judge for yourself...

Geoffrey and Maggie had been dating for five years when they decided to visit Knysna for a well-deserved holiday. They had heard that there were several excellent cycling routes in the area and so, being enthusiastic weekend cyclists, they brought their mountain bikes with them. Unbeknownst to each other, both Maggie and Geoffrey viewed this holiday as the means of resolving certain differing concerns they each individually had about their relationship.

Geoffrey had enjoyed a brief moment of glory in his late teens as the star of a provincial soccer team on a winning streak, but an unfortunate misstep on the pitch had led to a knee injury, which had put paid to his dreams of fame and fortune. At the time of the Knysna holiday, Geoffrey was stuck in a dead-end job teaching physical education at the local high school and coaching the local under-fifteen soccer team. Geoffrey had of late been concerned that Maggie's interest in him appeared to be waning and so he had the goal of re-awakening some of their initial ardour on their holiday. A friend had assured him that the forests in the area were extremely beautiful, secluded and romantic places, absolutely guaranteed to get any lady in the mood, and so Geoffrey hatched a plan to make full use of these purported benefits of the forest whilst on a cycling trail.

Maggie, on the other hand, was on an upward trajectory in her career, working long and hard hours as a corporate lawyer. At thirty-seven, the ticking of Maggie's biological clock was becoming deafening and she was seriously considering whether to end her relationship with Geoffrey, who showed no signs of popping the question and was possibly not the best genetic choice as father of her potential children. Maggie decided to use the opportunity of the unaccustomed leisure time on their holiday to clarify in her mind whether to stay with Geoffrey or not. Of course, she didn't share this goal with Geoffrey, and he, similarly, did not share his amorous ambitions with her.

On the morning in question, Geoffrey and an unsuspecting Maggie made an early start on the forest trail, which commenced on an open dirt road, but very rapidly led them deep into the ancient, unspoilt forest on their mountain bikes. And, certainly, Geoffrey's friend had not misled him - the route was breathtakingly beautiful. They cycled through densely forested valleys and gorges, the trail looping over several crystal-clear sepia-brown streams, stained that colour by tannins released into the water by fynbos, massive tree ferns and thick undergrowth fringing the river. The crowns of gigantic trees met overhead and they cycled through leafy tunnels, redolent with the vital, rich aromas of rotting leaves and fertile soil, serenaded by birdsong and the chatter of monkeys, high up in the forest canopy.

After an hour or two of cycling ever deeper and deeper into the forest, during which time Geoffrey and Maggie had not encountered a single other person, Geoffrey began to mentally prepare himself for what lay ahead. Maggie appeared to be in an excellent, really relaxed and receptive mood, and so he decided that the timing was perfect to put his plan into action. As they cycled into a beautiful, shady clearing in the forest, presided over by a massive, ancient Yellowwood tree, Geoffrey called to Maggie to stop for a break. Dismounting, they propped their bikes up against the Yellowwood tree and threw themselves down onto the forest floor, resting their aching muscles and slaking their thirst with the cold, clear, delicious stream water with which they had earlier filled their water bottles.

After a brief snack of dried fruit and nuts, Maggie lay back against a tree, closed her eyes and sighed deeply with satisfaction. Geoffrey realized that the perfect moment had arrived and he cleared his throat, *"Mags, I've got an idea,"* he said.

"Mmmnn?" Maggie mumbled, not opening her eyes.

Undaunted, Geoffrey tried again, *"Mags, listen, I've brought my camera. This place is just so beautiful and secluded and you're so gorgeous and... well, I kinda thought that perhaps you'd allow me to take some photos of you?"*

"What sort of photos?" asked Maggie, opening her eyes to squint suspiciously at Geoffrey. This wasn't the first time in the five years they had been together that Geoffrey had made this sort of suggestion to her and she had a fairly good idea of where this was going.

"Well... I thought I could take some very tasteful nude pics of you, Mags. You know... the contrast of your skin against the deep green of the forest would be simply gorgeous and we could enjoy looking at the pictures together. It could be quite exciting, actually, don't you think?" Maggie pursed her lips as Geoffrey's voice became a little squeaky in his race to finish what he wanted to say before she could jump in and turn him down.

"Geoff, really, I don't think..." she began, but Geoffrey had thoroughly rehearsed his arguments and he interrupted with,

"Mags, there's nobody around for miles – it's just you and me and this beautiful place and it would be so much fun. And besides, we're not going to be young forever and we should capture our youth and beauty on film whilst we still have it and you went to so much effort to lose all that weight

and you're looking so lovely and let's celebrate that and also, you can take pics of me too!"

Geoffrey had chosen his arguments well, as Maggie was extremely proud of her recent, hard-won weight loss and enjoyed showing off her body for the first time in years. In addition, she had lately been feeling that her youth was passing her by and had expressed her determination to seize the day and enjoy every moment of their youth whilst they still could. Maggie's extremely expressive face informed Geoffrey that his arguments were taking effect and so, in order to press his advantage home, he added, " *Come on, Mags, it will be something to tell our grandchildren about!*" This was a very sneaky strategy as he knew that Maggie was desperate to have children and that, by mentioning grandchildren, he was significantly raising his stakes with Maggie.

"*Oh, what the hell! Why not? Let's do it – let's have some fun!*" exclaimed Maggie and, in typical Maggie fashion, she immediately jumped up and began throwing off all her clothing, whilst Geoffrey, who couldn't quite believe how successful his strategies had proven to be, scrabbled in his daypack for his camera.

Modesty requires that we draw the curtain on the activities of the next fun-filled hour, but, suffice it to say, an uninhibited, rollicking great time was had by both Maggie and Geoffrey! Lying together afterwards on a bed of dried leaves, gazing up into the leafy canopy above their heads, Maggie sighed again with contentment. "*What a simply beautiful day!*" Closing her eyes she remarked, "*Isn't it strange how much more of the forest one experiences when you close your eyes? Try it, Geoff. Somehow your other senses seem to work so much better when your eyes are closed.*"

Geoffrey, ever the opportunist, and feeling extremely buoyed by the success of his previous ploys, said, "*Well, how about we play a little game, then? We'll blindfold you and then you can move around, simply experiencing the forest and see if you can sense your way towards me.*" Maggie thought this sounded like fun and so, without further ado, Geoffrey tied his bandanna around her eyes, turned her around a few times for good measure and let go of her. Then he crept away as silently as he could and hid behind a large bush a few metres from the clearing.

For the first ten minutes or so, Geoffrey crouched in his leafy bower, gleefully re-living the wonderful experiences of the past hour. He was sure that this would mark a turning point in his relationship with Maggie. He had never before experienced her in quite such a playful mood, and the memories, not to mention the photographs, would provide fuel for his imagination for some time to come. He decided that there were all kinds of new experiences that he would suggest to Maggie in future...

After a while Geoffrey began to wonder what had become of Maggie. He realized that he had been so caught up in his thoughts and memories that he had not paid attention to the fact that he hadn't heard a single sound from Maggie for some time. Thinking that he would change the game somewhat and sneak up on her for another helping of fun, Geoffrey crept out from behind his bush and looked around for Maggie. What he saw next chilled the very marrow of his bones and made his blood run cold with horror.

When Geoffrey related his experiences of that day to me, his pallor became even more pronounced and his wide, staring eyes began darting wildly from side-to-side. His white-knuckled hand clenching his glass was shaking so much that he began spilling beer all over the counter and I feared that he was in the grip of some kind of a fit. His raised voice started to draw attention from the other patrons and I put a hand on his forearm in an attempt to calm him down. Gradually, in fits and starts, I was able to piece together the story of what Geoffrey had witnessed that day in the forest clearing.

Maggie was standing, naked and blindfolded, in the centre of the clearing, her arms wrapped around the trunk of a massive tree, in which she was completely enfolded; a tree which had definitely not been there at the beginning of the game! A tree that she appeared, against all logic and reason, to be kissing. As Geoffrey watched in horror, a branch of the tree "grew" down Maggie's naked back and lovingly wrapped itself around her naked buttocks. A leafy green tendril twined through her hair to caress her cheek and a lustful moan escaped Maggie's lips.

Geoffrey screamed, "*Maggie! What the...*" and the apparition immediately disappeared, leaving Maggie sprawled on all fours in front of Geoffrey. "*Maggie, what on Earth... what was that thing?*" he screamed. Maggie very slowly lifted her head to look up at Geoffrey through her long lashes and the most evil, knowing smile curled her lips, as an emerald green glint briefly sparked in her normally deep-brown eyes.

The rest of the story Geoffrey delivered in a flat monotone. Maggie was changed forever by her experience in the forest. She stopped speaking to Geoffrey altogether and appeared to be entranced and inhabiting a magical world of her own. She left her job, sold all her possessions and moved to a small, hippy commune on the edge of the Knysna forest, where she remains to this day, living in a teepee. Geoffrey told me that he visited Maggie every year in an attempt to persuade her to return to him and to her former life. The horror of what he had witnessed that day in the forest remained as vivid to him as ever and he was of the opinion that he would never, ever get over it. But he hoped that by getting Maggie back he would find some healing. The day I met him marked the fifth anniversary of those horrific events, but Geoffrey was no closer to getting Maggie to change her mind about him, or even to acknowledge his existence.

I mused to myself that Geoffrey and Maggie had certainly both had a transformative experience in the forest, but I wasn't convinced that it had been a positive one for either of them.

This story, though strange enough, has a final twist to the tale. A few weeks after my encounter with Geoffrey in the pub, I happened to mention the story at a barbeque, hosted by newly-acquired friends. A forestry official at the barbeque indicated that he had heard about Maggie and Geoffrey's story and that he had additional information to add.

It seems that the clearing that Geoffrey had chosen for his photo shoot was, unbeknownst to him, equipped with several motion-activated cameras, which had been installed by the Department of Forestry in order to capture pictures of the local wild life. The following is a re-creation of the events in the office shared by Sarel Basson and Giel Coetzee, local foresters, when they browsed through the developed photos.

"Hey Sarel. Look here man! Seems like some idiots decided to get down-and-dirty and take porn pics in the forest! Check it out!"

"Nee, sies man!⁴ Some people have no manners, hey? Also, a bit disrespectful of the forest, don't you think? And the leopard could have got them while they were messing around in the nude! Check, the woman's got a nice body though. Hey, what's that there in the last photo, Gielie?"

"Let me see... no man, must be dirt on the camera lens or something. That chick must be playing some game, hey? She's just standing there with her arms in the air and her lips pursed like she's kissing someone. But the photo's all blurry, man. There's a green and brown blur all around her body. Damn shame that, would have been a really nice pic, otherwise. Fine looking woman, though what she's doing with that poor loser is anyone's guess..."

---

4   An expression of disgust in Afrikaans.

Chapter 12
The Importance of Roots

At a small local art gallery, I encountered the original work of Greta van Niekerk, a rather mysterious and reclusive artist I had read about in a magazine some time before my visit to Knysna. Her work had gained considerable international acclaim, and art aficionados in the know were of the opinion that her star was ascending. It appeared that investing in her work was a wise decision and I would have done so had my career and finances not been on such shaky ground at the time.

The photographs of her work that had appeared in the magazine I had read didn't even begin to do justice to the powerful emotions that the actual work evoked in me. Standing spellbound in the Knysna art gallery, what struck me most forcefully about Greta's work was the sharp contrast between her work done prior to 2005 and the paintings she completed subsequently. Before 2005, Greta exclusively painted small, dead creatures in tones of sepia, dust and ash. Although the paintings were profoundly sad; some might even call them morbid; they certainly evoked a powerful, visceral response in the viewer. I was absolutely transfixed by a painting of a tiny dead bird, which had obviously recently emerged from the egg, the shards of which lay scattered about, the weak, vulnerable little body covered in damp feathers. The bird was held, with infinite tenderness in the left palm of a disembodied hand, whereas the right palm cupped an intact egg. I was almost overwhelmed by the pathos of the contrast between the hopeful fecundity of the egg and the hopelessness of that tiny, dead body. Other paintings depicted, respectively, a cracked clay bowl spilling a pile of dead grasshoppers onto the sand, a pile of small, dead fish in a dried-up pond and a tiny dead kitten with a toy between its paws, its head at an unnatural angle.

In stark contrast, Greta's paintings after 2005 were wild and exuberant abstracts on large canvasses, absolutely bursting with life and colour and vitality. What a remarkable metamorphosis! There was absolutely no doubt in my mind that the artist had undergone a powerful personal transformation and, as such, I found her story to be irresistible.

I attempted to gain an interview with Greta van Niekerk, but her telephone number was unlisted and she clearly did not engage in the usual social media activities that often enable one to track people. Greta's agent in Cape Town, as well as the city galleries normally exhibiting her work, refused to oblige, saying that Greta did not grant interviews to anyone whatsoever, as she believed that her work said absolutely everything she had ever needed, or wanted, to say. Much disheartened, I spent some time in the Knysna gallery, gazing at her work and trying to get into the mind of the artist.

The rather chatty and slightly bored curator of the local gallery was able to assist me somewhat in my quest to get to know Greta. She was able to supply the information that Greta van Niekerk had moved to Knysna in 2004 after a personal tragedy and that she lived in a very remote place, up in the mountains. The local curator repeated the information that the other galleries had supplied, namely that Greta never, ever granted interviews.

I gave up on the story of Greta van Niekerk at that point and continued pursuing other stories for my book. However, a month later, fate was to intervene in the most unexpected way in order to bring me a wonderfully inspiring tale.

During my time in Knysna I indulged my love of hiking on a regular basis. How could I resist, given the wild and natural beauty of the place? On one particular morning I had almost completed a six-and-a-half kilometre hike that wended through dense, indigenous forests to emerge at a lovely, secluded picnic spot, where I had planned to enjoy an early lunch. Hearing a soft whimpering sound in the bushes to my left just off the path, I stooped to investigate, finding a small, tan, miniature Dachshund quivering with fear and licking its left paw. I held my hand out to the terrified dog and he licked my fingers, clearly deciding that I was to be trusted. I picked up the small dog and sat down on a log to examine its paw. There was nothing seriously wrong, just a large thorn embedded in the paw pad and, apart from a sharp yelp when I extracted the thorn, the dog appeared mostly unscathed by the experience. When I put him down on the ground, he took a few tentative steps on his injured paw and then, finding it to be fine, jumped up against my leg and licked my arm. I gave him some water, which he lapped thirstily and a piece of egg sandwich from my picnic, which he gobbled down. Now, of course, I had to decide what to do with the little fellow. Scratching him behind the ears, I said softly, "*Where's your family, little guy? Did you get lost on the trail?*" The dog whined and pricked up his ears.

Then I too heard what had attracted his attention. A soft woman's voice calling, "*Dash... Dash... where are you, my little one?"* I picked up the dog and briskly walked in the direction of the woman's voice, further down the trail.

As I rounded a loop in the trail I saw her: a tiny, delicate, ethereal-looking creature with an extremely worried expression on her face, which disappeared as her face lit up with joy to see her dog. *"Dash! There you are! Where have you been, you little rascal? I've been looking for you all morning!"* Dash madly wagged his tail and struggled to get out of my arms and so I put him down on the ground and he raced up to his mistress for a joyful reunion. *"Where did you find him?"* the woman asked me, *"I was frantic. He took off after a bushbuck and I thought I'd lost him forever."* Her voice broke slightly on the last sentence and I could see that the little dog meant the world to her. When I told her about the thorn I had removed from Dash's paw, she grasped my right hand between her two, small soft hands, looked deep into my eyes and softly said, *"Thank you,"* but with such heartfelt gratitude, that it suffused my entire being with joy.

On an impulse I invited the woman and Dash to share my picnic lunch and her moment's hesitation before responding in the affirmative told me that she wasn't accustomed to the company of others but that she would make an exception due to the circumstances of our meeting. I introduced myself to her and nearly fell over backwards in surprise when she reciprocated saying, *"Greta van Niekerk."* Her wry smile at my surprise confirmed for me that she was well aware of the impact upon me of her name. However, I didn't comment and refrained from asking her about her work, even though I was dying to hear her story. Some instinct informed me to proceed with extreme caution around this shy, introverted person.

Once seated at a wooden picnic table and enjoying egg mayonnaise sandwiches, Greta asked me what I was doing in Knysna. She had already noticed from my vehicle registration plates that I was not a local. I took great care in presenting my work to her in the best possible light and when she asked about the stories, I related one or two to her, with relish. When I paused for breath, Greta remarked, "*You are a natural story-teller, Mr. Allen. I can imagine that the world of journalism didn't really feed your soul. I would love to read some of your stories for myself. Would you consider allowing me to do so?*" I was rather taken aback at the astuteness of her comments. I was feeling a little bit protective of my stories at that point and hesitated to share them with anyone else until they had been polished and perfected. Greta remained perfectly still, watching me intently with her wise, black eyes set in their network of fine wrinkles and patiently waited for me to reach a decision.

"*Yes. I would like that,*" I replied, surprising myself. Somehow I knew that I could trust this strange, fey woman and, besides, there was just a feeling of such rightness about her request that I simply couldn't refuse.

And so it was that, a few days later, I dropped off eight of my stories at Greta's tiny cottage, which was surprisingly ramshackle for an artist of her stature. We made an appointment to meet there again a week hence, at which time she would share her first impressions of my work.

At our appointment, Greta astounded me with her wisdom and insight and I was incredibly pleased that she had been my very first reader. She had, in a few short hours, immeasurably enriched my work. Her comment, at the very end of our discussion, is one that I most treasure to this day. "*Peter, I know that the Lady will be pleased with your work.*

You have done her justice." Then, just as I was preparing to leave, Greta placed her hand on my arm to stop me and said, *"Peter, I have a story to tell. Perhaps it could be included in your wonderful book?"* Well, as you can imagine, my heart nearly burst open with excitement and so I sat right down again and took out my notepad and pen. This, then, is Greta's story.

Greta was born into an extremely wealthy family, which had made their money over three generations from the manufacture of precision instruments for industrial and laboratory use. As the youngest of three children, the only daughter and of an artistic, rather than a business bent, she had never felt seen or understood by the other members of her family. Both her older brothers took after their father and were large, powerful, forceful extroverts. They delighted in playing elaborate pranks on Greta and bullied her whenever they believed they could get away with it, which was often, as Greta's parents were great believers in the old adage that, *"boys will be boys"*. Greta, who was always small, quiet and introverted and not at all adept at standing up for herself, often felt as if she disappeared entirely when her family was around. Greta's mother's life revolved around supporting and nurturing her sons and her husband. She and her daughter were never close. Greta's brothers were top achievers from the very beginning and they both ended up with MBA's from a prestigious school, whereas Greta struggled to concentrate or to apply herself at school and just drifted along in a dream world without making waves and without being noticed much at all. When Greta was twenty-one, her maternal grandmother provided the funds and the impetus for her granddaughter to study fine art at college, which is what she herself had studied many years earlier. Had she not, Greta would probably never have discovered what it was that she wanted to do with her life.

As it was, at college Greta finally discovered her passion. She simply loved her course and when she was painting or drawing, the entire world suddenly made sense. She found that she was able to express herself through her art in a way that simply wasn't possible through words alone. And she also discovered that when she spoke through her art, people actually listened, which they very rarely did when she spoke in words. Greta won a prestigious award for her final year exhibition and a great future was predicted for her. None of her family made the effort to attend her prize-winning exhibition and, although she told herself that it didn't matter, deep within she felt sad and unlovable.

It was around this time that Greta met Sam at the home of a mutual friend. Sam was five years older and an attorney. She was a powerful, opinionated, ambitious woman who swept Greta right off her feet and she fell very deeply in love. When Greta finally, after almost six months of dating Sam, introduced Sam to her family, they were horrified. Greta's father informed her that she was unnatural, a disgrace to the family and no longer welcome in his home. Greta's mother simply bowed her head and quietly accepted her husband's decision. Although Greta's brothers did call to check up on her from time-to-time, it was pretty much the end of all contact with her family. To tell the truth, she hardly missed them and she was financially secure, due to a trust fund from her grandmother that ensured that she would never have to earn a living for the rest of her life.

Greta and Sam were very happy for the next ten years. Although Greta enjoyed the stable and secure home life they created together, she was unable to find any direction in her art. She started, and destroyed, hundreds of artworks during this time. It appeared as if her early promise was doomed to remain unfulfilled. To Greta it felt as if she was waiting for something to happen; something that would provide her with inspiration or with a purpose to her life. Sam often expressed frustration at Greta's lack of direction and her aimless drifting, but it was probably partly this lack of ambition on Greta's part that kept them together for so long. Sam would not have been able to handle the competition had Greta been successful. Sam needed to always be the centre of attention and the top dog and Greta was very happy for her to occupy this role, as long as she, Greta, could simply drift along, undisturbed, in her little dream world.

When Greta was thirty-six, she and Sam made the decision to have a baby together. Greta had had a pelvic infection when she was a child, which had left her infertile, and so the couple made the decision that Sam would be the one to carry their child, even though she was already over forty by this time. The women very carefully selected the father of their child from the hundreds of options available to them and, within two months of being artificially inseminated, Sam was pregnant. What followed was the most wonderful time for Greta. She and Sam had never been closer and Sam appeared to become softened by impending motherhood. She was kinder and gentler with Greta, who absolutely blossomed in the warm light of her partner's love. Then, six months into the pregnancy, disaster struck.

Sam was about to enter the court to present closing arguments on a case that she had been working on for months, when she was gripped by a sudden fierce pain in her pelvis. She bent over double, gasping with pain and fear and reached out to her colleague for assistance. Eight hours later, despite the very best medical attention, Sam was delivered of a dead baby, which signalled the death knell for her relationship with Greta too. Somehow, their partnership was not able to survive this tragedy and two months later Sam left Greta in a whirlwind of tears and recriminations. In the aftermath of Sam's departure Greta was left shell-shocked and disbelieving. How had her life fallen apart so rapidly? Sam's devastation at the loss of their child had, of course, taken centre stage, leaving Greta now time or space in which to grieve. So, after Sam left, Greta spent the next six months all alone and completely isolated, silently grieving the loss of both her child and the love of her life.

One morning Greta got out of bed, walked barefoot over to the blank, stretched canvas that had been waiting on her easel for more than a year and began mixing paints. Ten hours later she suddenly became aware of the fact that she was dizzy with hunger, quivering with exhaustion and that her pyjamas were covered in paint spatters. But, there before her on the easel, was the genesis of the very first painting she had made since leaving college that accurately expressed her feelings. It was eventually to become the painting of the little dead bird that I had first admired in the gallery in Knysna. During the next few weeks, as she painted in a frenzy of creativity, Greta found that she was resenting more-and-more the intrusion upon her life and her painting that friends, her brothers, newspapers, the mail and her neighbours represented. And so she decided to sell her large city house, which anyway reminded her too powerfully of happier times, and move to a remote cottage in the mountains of Knysna. The reason she chose Knysna was simply that she knew that it was a small, quiet town and also because her grandmother had always spoken of the place with great fondness. Greta was far too distracted by her muse to spend much time considering which town would best suit her, other than that it should be both small and quiet. The cottage she found was in a state of some disrepair, but to Greta that mattered not a whit. It was extremely quiet and remote and the surrounding mountains and forests were perfectly suited to encourage creative endeavours.

For the next couple of years, Greta lived only to paint. She expressed all of her hurt and sadness and loneliness and grief on the canvasses that rapidly piled up in her makeshift studio in the sunny sitting room of the little cottage. She went for weeks on end without seeing a single other person and her infrequent sorties down to town to buy supplies became a trial and an unwelcome distraction from the business of painting. She became somewhat eccentric, painting in her underwear in summer and wrapped in a bathrobe in winter. Her clothing became shabby and everything she owned was covered in paint. She lost what little extra weight she had been carrying and became thin and insubstantial, drifting through her dream world of creativity, disconnected from reality and accompanied only by her muse.

One spring morning, Greta awoke naked and freezing cold on the floor of her studio, her face and hair covered in brown and grey paint from where she had fallen asleep on her palette. The last thing she could remember was painting, with the windows thrown wide open, to relish the rainstorm of the previous night. A tiny, but insistent, voice inside her mind told her that she had gone too far and she realized, with considerable shock, that she was actually slowly dying. She knew that she had to make a decision about whether she wanted to live or not and that it was not a foregone conclusion what that decision would be. She hacked the dried oil paints out of her hair with the kitchen scissors and then shaved her head, took a shower and dressed in marginally clean clothing before sitting down to tea and toast, the first meal she could recall eating in quite some time. Instead of returning to her easel, Greta pulled on a fleece hoodie and went for a walk in her wet, overgrown garden.

As she walked past an enormous, lush bush covered in a profusion of purple flowers, Greta glanced down and noticed how very rich and fertile the black soil appeared. A stray thought crossed her mind that just about anything could grow in that soil. On an impulse, she bent down and thrust both her hands deep into the moist, humus-rich soil, curling her fingers around and squeezing the damp, cool solidity of it. She closed her eyes and breathed deeply of the fecund scent of the soil and the wet garden and it occurred to her that she felt happy for the first time in a very long while.

Greta's hands began to tingle pleasurably and she wriggled them even deeper into the soil. Suddenly it felt as if her fingers were extending and her eyes popped open in shock. She gasped to discover that her hands had indeed become tree roots that were rapidly stretching and growing as they worked their way deep into the soil, seeking moisture and sustenance.

"*Don't be afraid,*" Greta heard a soft, gentle voice speaking deep within her heart and she looked up to see a lovely green woman smiling down at her. Dumbstruck, Greta could only stare at the woman as she spoke again, "*Greta, you* are allowing yourself to drift away from life and yet you have such a good reason for being here, for being alive. You have been given an exceptional talent, which allows you to move the hearts of people and to make the world a better place and yet you don't share that talent. You choose not to nourish or sustain yourself and yet you live in a place where so much nourishment is freely available for the taking. Feel your roots, Greta, feel how they reach deep into the soil, absorbing sustenance and hydrating themselves with the water of life. Greta, roots are so very important." As the green woman spoke, Greta felt her roots stretch out far and wide and these roots provided a conduit for the sustenance that her body required to slowly, gently, unfold into a strong and beautiful tree. The feeling of connection and nurturing was far beyond anything that Greta had ever encountered in her lonely, disconnected existence thus far.

"You are noticing how connected you feel, Greta. Your roots connect you with all the other trees and plants around you via an incredibly intricate web of symbiotic, mycorrhizal fungi, which allow all the plants to communicate with each other. As you grow, notice how many other living things are attracted to you, and so arrive to come and co-create with you." Greta became aware of insects buzzing around her crown, birds settling on her branches and then a small, grey doe shyly appeared and began to delicately nibble at her leaves. Various species of moss and fungi and lichens began to grow on her trunk and around her roots and she gradually became aware of the micro-organisms in the soil that were growing and multiplying and supplying her with nourishment, just as she provided them with vital sugars and other compounds that they required for their growth.

"Do you see, Greta, that you are a part of a great and grand co-creation with all other living creatures? You are connected to Life, and your strength and survival are dependent upon being part of the whole and contributing all that you are to the whole. You are not alone. You have never been alone. You have only imagined that you were disconnected and alone. Don't you realize that even your inspiration as an artist comes from being part of the All? When you paint, you are tapping into the collective creativity of which you are a part. This is your purpose, Greta. To simply express, in your own unique way, that unique perspective which is you. To express it as beautifully and magnificently and grandly as you possibly can. This is your gift to All That Is, and this is your reason for being." Greta felt her heart swell with joy and wonder at the words of the Green Lady and then she simply relished the ecstasy of her connection with Life.

Some time later she gradually became aware of the fact that she was curled up in the overgrown flowerbed, clutching two handfuls of soil with a massive grin on her face!

"Something changed for me from that day onwards," Greta told me. "Something clicked into place and I stopped grieving. The lifting of my sadness and depression made me realize that, for my entire life, I had barely been alive. Now, I wanted to live and to experience life to the full. And I wanted to paint and to share my work with the world. I found myself an agent and the rest, as they say, is history. Except, of course, for my precious little Dash coming into my life for companionship and also to make sure that I am reminded to stay in place, rooted to the Earth!"

Greta's story struck a very deep chord within me. I too had been feeling lonely and disconnected from the world for some time. I knew that I could follow Greta's example and also connect with the life force within, thereby finding my own way towards a more authentic version of myself. Suddenly my old life and my job at the newspaper seemed very far away, and just that little bit meaningless. I felt a shiver of excitement run up my spine. What would the future hold for me? Could a deeply transformative experience be awaiting me as well?

CHAPTER 13
THE PURPOSE OF SUFFERING

One of the first places I visited when I arrived in Knysna was Karatara, a small settlement about thirty kilometres from Sedgefield, the closest town to Knysna. I had heard about South Africa's first free rural eco-business school for entrepreneurs was based in the Karatara settlement, and the journalist in me sensed a good story. However, the story that eventually found me there had nothing whatsoever to do with business, but everything to do with the heart.

Karatara used to be a forestry station in the 1920's and became a settlement for forestry workers in the 1940's. There were fifty-three wooden houses in which black and mixed-race forestry workers, all of whom were employed by the National Department of Forestry, lived with their families in the so-called "bosdorp" (forest village). Karatara was eventually de-proclaimed as forestry land and, after much wrangling and several official investigations, the ownership of these houses was legally transferred to the historical occupiers in 2014.

Several of the inhabitants of these homes had benefited from the activities of the rural business school at Karatara[5] and had obtained a Certificate in Practical Business Administration. Some of these graduates had gone on to establish small eco-businesses, in harmony with their

---

5   The Eden campus of TSiBA (The Tertiary School in Business Administration), a private, not-for-profit business school founded in 2004 to "Ignite Opportunity" for entrepreneurs

environment and offering much-needed employment within the community. However, students also came from far further afield in South Africa, as the school offered full board and lodging for sixty-five non-local students for ten months of the year. I was impressed by the many activities and the successes of the school; however my story was to be found in the kitchen rather than in the classrooms.

I was served lunch in the school cafeteria by Martha, a current student at the school and a resident of the bosdorp. All students were obliged to contribute a certain amount of time to the upkeep of the school and the cafeteria was Martha's special responsibility. As I was leaving, I popped my head into the kitchen to thank Martha for the excellent lunch, and I noticed a small girl crouching in the corner of the kitchen with her head down on her knees, which were drawn up to her chest. She looked up at me as I called Martha's name and I was shocked to observe the extremely waxy pallor of her emaciated, café latte coloured face. *"Hello, who are you?"* I asked, crouching down next to the little girl, but she didn't answer, merely putting her head back down onto her knees with a listless and exhausted sigh.

"That's my daughter, Elsa," said Martha, her eyes clouding over with concern as she observed her little girl's posture.

"Is she OK?" I asked. I am not an expert on children, but I could sense that there was something very wrong with this child.

"*Dis bloedsiekte*," Martha whispered, with a slow, hopeless shaking of her head. To me "bloedsiekte" (blood sickness) could only translate to one thing, which was AIDS, and an icy dread ran down my spine to think that this beautiful child could be a victim to the virus which had wrecked the lives of so many South Africans. But then Martha showed me some leaflets that her doctor had given her and I realized that the child was the victim of acute lymphoblastic leukaemia, or cancer of the white blood cells in the bone marrow.

Martha sank down onto a chair in the kitchen and sobbed as she poured out her tale of woe. It seemed that little Elsa, who was six years old, had started complaining of pains in her joints a few months earlier. The child was listless, weak and pale and she refused to eat. She also had a fever. Martha had thought that Elsa had caught the flu, which was doing the rounds at the time, and so she put Elsa to bed with some aspirin and coaxed her into eating chicken broth several times a day. But Elsa just didn't get any better and when Martha noticed several unexplained bruises on Elsa's body and tiny red spots under her skin, she began to feel concerned and she took Elsa to the local clinic. The doctor who examined Elsa at the clinic immediately referred her to a specialist in George, the nearest city to Knysna. As Martha's family did not have the means of taking Elsa to George, not to mention, afford the fees of a specialist, the director of the school offered to help in exchange for extra duties for Martha at some time in the future when Elsa was once again healthy.

What followed was a confusing and upsetting whirl of medical examinations, blood work, scans and even a bone marrow biopsy, all of which finally confirmed that Elsa had leukaemia and that she would probably die within a few months if she was not provided with proper treatment. Elsa would need to spend prolonged periods of time at the hospital in George to receive chemotherapy, which would continue for more than three years. Other therapies might also be needed, the goal being to induce in Elsa a lasting remission, defined as the absence of detectable cancer cells in the body, the specialist had explained to Martha. However, it was crucial to get the treatment started as soon as possible if Elsa was to have any chance at survival. The diagnosis had been received two weeks earlier, and Martha was still in a state of shock. She was well aware of the fact that there was no way she would ever be able to afford the treatment that Elsa required and the school would not be able to continue assisting at the level which would be required for the foreseeable future. The situation seemed hopeless.

I left Karatara in a gloomy and despondent mood. Elsa's beautiful, exhausted little face began haunting both my waking and sleeping hours. I wished that I could find a way to help her. One morning I awoke with the name of Helena Kroukamp on my lips. She was the journalist who had written the newspaper article that had provided me with some of the inspiration to start my book. Somehow I was certain that she could assist Elsa. I went to visit Helena in her modest offices in the centre of Knysna and watched her somewhat sharp face softening as I explained Elsa's situation to her. When I had finished she exclaimed, *"We need to crowdfund Elsa's treatment!"* I had never heard of the concept of crowdfunding before, but Helena explained to me that it was possible to access funding from hundreds, if not thousands, of ordinary, concerned people all over the world if one knew how best to use social media and online funding mechanisms. Helena immediately set about registering on a charity crowdfunding platform and creating a Facebook page for Elsa, which she populated with heart-rending photographs of the child, her family and her home, taken by a freelance photographer from whom she had called in a favour. She also wrote articles about Elsa's plight that appeared in all of the Garden Route newspapers and the local classifieds, the Action Ads. She accomplished this by feverishly working during her own free time and I assisted wherever I could, and learning a great deal in the process. The result of all this activity is that, within a month, Helena had managed to source sufficient funding to cover the cost of Elsa's first year of treatment and she was confident that the rest would follow shortly.

During the months of treatment that followed, I visited Elsa at least once a week at the hospital in George. Martha, who had been excused from her duties at the school and had had her studies deferred until she could once again fully focus on them, was provided with free temporary housing at the hospital residence and she spent most of her waking hours at Elsa's bedside.

The little girl was not doing at all well. It almost broke my heart to witness her small, deathly-pale bald head, fragile as a bird's egg, resting on her pillow and her painfully thin little body barely making a dent in the stark white bedclothes. She had had a portacath surgically implanted under the skin near her collar bone, through which drugs were administered. It caused me an almost physical pang to realize that this device was uncomfortable for her, as her little hand, with its nails bitten down to the quick, continuously fluttered near her collar bone.

Martha had told me that the doctor's major concern was with the increased risk of infection, particularly pneumonia, and that they were all on high alert for symptoms such as shortness of breath, chest pain, coughing or vomiting.

Elsa would have to remain in intensive care for the duration of her chemotherapy until the doctor believed that the risk of such infection had been minimised.

Against all odds, Elsa survived her first round of chemotherapy and, within a couple of weeks, was moved from intensive care to a general oncology ward. The little girl appeared much happier here and, for the first time, her eyes were bright and she was sitting upright and appeared alert and interested in her surroundings when I next visited her.

I arrived just as Martha was leaving to go and meet with Elsa's doctor en route to the store to purchase a few items that Elsa needed. She was, therefore, very happy to see me and said, as she was leaving, "*Elsa, tell Mr. Allen about your dream, my baby,*" and then she winked at me, blew a kiss at Elsa and left. It was good to see Martha in a playful mood for once, thanks to the improvement in her little girl's health.

I bent down to kiss Elsa's cheek and she grabbed my hand and whispered in my ear, "*It wasn't a dream, you know.*"

"*Really?*" I said, settling down into the chair at the side of the bed. "*Why don't you tell me all about it?*" The story that followed would probably have been dismissed by any rational adult as a dream or fantasy at best and a delusion or even a drug-induced hallucination at worst. The story was, however, extremely interesting to me for reasons that will become obvious below.

Elsa had been feeling really sad and homesick the previous day. Although she had started to feel a bit better, she was really missing her friends and the rest of her family. But most of all she missed the forest surrounding her home. It had always been her best friend, her refuge and her playground, and the sterile, bright white environment in which she found herself was cold and unfriendly. After Elsa's mother had tucked her in, read her a story and then left for the night, Elsa had started quietly sobbing, thinking about how lonely she was feeling and how much she wanted to go home to the forest.

Suddenly Elsa heard an unfamiliar, barely audible, scratching sound outside her window and so she climbed out of her bed and pulled the curtain aside. To her astonishment she saw a large Eagle Owl perched on her window sill. The owl stared straight into Elsa's eyes, slowly blinked a couple of times and then she heard a deep voice resonating within her heart. *"Elsa, come with me,"* the owl hooted.

"But... But I can't," she replied, *"I'm sick and I'm not supposed to get out of bed. Also, my mother told me not to talk to strangers."*

"Elsa, what does your heart tell you? Am I a stranger to you?" asked the owl, his large orange eyes staring deep into her own.

*"Uh, no, I guess not, "*Elsa replied, as she realised that she actually knew this owl very well. She had seen him several times in the trees near her home and often heard him who-whooing before she fell asleep at night.

"And the very reason that you need to come with me is because you're sick," the owl continued. *"We're going someplace that will make you feel much better."*

"Uh, OK," said Elsa. *"But how are we going to get there and won't my mother be sad when she arrives tomorrow morning and I'm not here?"*

"Elsa, we're going to fly there and we'll be back before morning. Nobody will even know that we've gone," replied the owl. *"Now, open the window and climb out onto the window sill."* Elsa did what the owl told her. She found that she wasn't at all afraid, even though her hospital room

was on the third floor of the building. *"Now climb onto my back and hold on tight!"* hooted the owl. Elsa was amazed to discover that she was quite small enough now to fit comfortably onto the owl's back and so she held tightly onto his feathers as he who-whooed once or twice and then silently flew off the window sill into the dark night.

The flight was absolutely exhilarating as the owl dived and swooped and then flew at top speed and Elsa nestled deeper into his feathers for warmth. Finally they arrived at their destination, which turned out to be the forests in which Elsa had grown up. The owl swooped to a halt in a forest clearing, the full moon lighting their way and causing a silvery glistening on the leaves of the trees and bushes that surrounded them. *"I'm home!"* Elsa crowed, as she breathed deeply of the familiar scents of fertile, humus-rich, moist soil and green leafy growth. *"But, what are we going to do here?"* she asked, *"It's late and my family and friends must be asleep. They won't want to play with me now and they might tell my mother and then I'd get into trouble for getting out of my bed,"* she said with a worried frown.

"You're going to meet with your forest family tonight, little one," replied the owl.

"But, where are they?" asked Elsa, glancing around the empty clearing in the forest.

"Do you see those two tall trees over there?" asked the owl. Elsa nodded. *"Well, they are the door to a wonderful world, just beyond this one. That is where we are going tonight."* The owl led Elsa to the trees and then encouraged her to step between them. For a moment Elsa could see nothing at all, only a strange, silvery mist that swirled all around her. But then, as she took another few steps, the mist

cleared and she found herself in the most wonderful place she could ever have imagined.

She was in a forest glade, but the trees surrounding her were truly gigantic and absolutely covered in tiny, multi-coloured, twinkling lights. Looking closer at the lights, she saw that they were actually tiny, perfectly-formed, beautiful little creatures in brightly-coloured clothing, darting through the leaves in a wild, joyful dance. *"Oh! Look, it's fairies!"* gasped Elsa, her eyes widening in amazement. There were larger creatures with a variety of animal faces dancing in a double circle in the clearing, bobbing and weaving amongst each other in a chaotic dance that kept resolving into complex patterns. In the centre of the two circles was a tall, lovely, green woman. As Elsa stared, transfixed, at the sights before her, the circles of dancers parted to form a double line and the Green Lady glided between the dancers up to Elsa and held out her hand. *"Are you the fairy queen?"* whispered Elsa in awe, but still taking the Lady's hand without a second's hesitation.

"I'm the spirit of the forest," the Lady replied as she led Elsa into the dance. To Elsa's complete surprise, she found that she knew all the steps to the dance. She twirled and jumped and danced and whirled, realizing that she felt completely healthy and well in a way that she hadn't felt for a very long time. The music grew louder and faster until Elsa's cheeks were pink from exertion and her hair swung out behind her in a wild tangle.

Then, finally, the dance ended and the dancers made their way, with much excited laughing and chattering, to the long tables to the side of the clearing. The tables were absolutely laden with tempting food displayed on leaves, and large acorns filled with a sparkling pink drink, which Elsa immediately sampled as she was so thirsty from all the dancing. She had never tasted anything so delicious in all her life! It tasted like liquid sunshine and ripe peaches and happiness. She felt a warm, golden glow suffusing her entire being as she finished her drink and immediately had another. Then, wiping her mouth with the back of her hand, she sampled a little pink cake frosted with lavender icing and covered in tiny silver sparkles. It was divine and she closed her eyes in delight as she tasted blueberry ice cream and perfume and spring meadows. The Green Lady appeared at her side, smiling. *"You're enjoying our feast, I see,"* she said.

"I've never tasted anything like it!" replied Elsa, biting into a pale green cake that tasted of toffee apples and holidays. *"I'm just so hungry!"* exclaimed Elsa, grabbing yet another cake, which was orange and covered in tiny golden sparkles.

After eating and drinking her fill, Elsa sat down on a tree stump covered with soft, bright-green moss and listened to the music played by the fairy musicians. Just like the voice of the Lady, she could hear the music directly in her heart, instead of through her ears. The music sounded like laughter and crystal-clear running water and tiny glass bells and it made Elsa feel deeply and completely happy and content. The Green Lady sat behind her and plaited tiny white flowers into her hair.

"Who are all these creatures?" Elsa asked the Green Lady.

"They're called sylphs," the Lady answered. *"They make sure that the trees and the flowers grow properly and remain happy and healthy."*

"I wish that I had a sylph to make me healthy again," whispered Elsa sadly, the corners of her mouth drooping as her bottom lip quivered.

The Lady hugged her close and told her, "You do, you know! Your body has a spirit being who looks after you and makes sure that things are all going according to the plan that you decided on even before you were born."

"Well, where is my sylph then?" asked Elsa indignantly. "She's not doing a very good job because when I'm not here in this place I'm normally quite sick, you know."

"I know," affirmed the Lady, with infinite gentleness and compassion. "But you know, Elsa, you are much more than you think you are. You believe that you are just a sick little girl, but you are actually a powerful and magnificent spirit being who has decided to allow a little part of itself to forget what it truly is and pretend to be Elsa for a little while. This being loves you, Elsa, far more than anyone here on Earth could ever love you; far more even than you love yourself. You will become this being when you aren't pretending to be limited as you are here on Earth, and when you leave Earth you will once again remember who you truly are. This being decided, before it expressed a part of itself to be born as you, Elsa, that it would choose to go through some hardships and experience some pain and suffering for a very short while for some very good reasons, which you will remember when you leave this place. I don't know what your reasons were, but, for some people, suffering and hardships make them strong and help them to grow in love and compassion so that they can do even more incredible things later on."

"What is it that I must do later?" wondered Elsa, "And will it be when I am a grown-up?"

"Only you will know that, Elsa, and only a little later. It might even be when you are in another life, not as Elsa, but as someone else. But when it is time, you will know exactly what it is that you must do. And believe me, it will be something very wonderful that will make a beautiful difference in the world," said the Lady.

Elsa leaned back and sighed deeply. "I want to help people and to make a difference, especially to other children who are also sick," she said, "It's just so hard sometimes to be in the hospital and to feel miserable and weak all the time."

"That is why you need to come back here and spend some time with us, every now and then," said the Lady, "So you can also have some time to feel well and to enjoy yourself. Then the sickness won't be quite as hard to bear."

"Oh, does that mean I'm coming back here again?" asked Elsa in excitement. "Can I come back again tomorrow night?"

"Perhaps not tomorrow night, but very soon," replied the Lady.

"Oh good," said Elsa, sighing with contentment. "I'm having so much fun," she whispered, her eyes beginning to flutter shut with exhaustion. It had been a very long, eventful evening for the little girl.

Elsa didn't remember the trip back to the hospital at all, but when she opened her eyes, she was back in her hospital bed and the nurse was placing her breakfast on a tray in front of her. To her surprise, she was very hungry and, for the first time in weeks, she ate all of her food.

Elsa was to make several more visits to the forest glade during her time in the hospital. Most weeks when I visited she would have some delightful, new story to tell me. I began to really look forward to our visits so that I could hear about Elsa's latest adventures in the forest. She had stopped telling anyone else about her forest visits as they all believed that she had only been dreaming, but Elsa knew that I took her stories seriously. So seriously, in fact, that one day I asked Elsa to give the Green Lady a message from me. *"Please would you ask the Lady if I will ever meet her myself,"* I requested of Elsa.

To my utter delight, the following week Elsa had a message for me from the Green Lady. *"The Lady asked me to tell you that it is no mistake that all of these stories about her are finding their way to you,"* Elsa said, screwing up her eyes as she attempted to recall the Lady's exact words. *"As you make the choice to open your heart, more stories will arrive and, when you are ready, you will meet the Lady for yourself."* A chill ran up my spine as I heard these words. I was convinced that these were not the words of a six-year old child, but rather a message for me from the Lady herself. I found myself looking forward with great anticipation to my time remaining in Knysna.

In the meantime, Elsa's stories of her visits in the forest with the Green Lady were an absolute delight for me to hear. She told me about a daytime visit in which she helped the forest spirits to build a tree house, which they decorated by making vines and flowers rapidly entwine into beautiful, living wall art. On another occasion, she swam by the light of the moon in a mysterious rock pool surrounded by ferns and moss-covered pebbles, with tiny luminous fish nibbling at her toes in the silvery water. She described to me a midnight picnic, high up in the topmost branches of a gigantic tree draped in old mans' beard, from which the sylphs taught her to fly, using thoughts alone. On one occasion she rode on the back of a massive stag in a wild chase through the forest, accompanied by hundreds of other creatures, just for the sheer exhilaration of it. And the feasts! Elsa had never before eaten such amazing and wonderful food and could spend hours just relating to me the taste sensations that she had experienced. I had no way of proving that the visits were real – they could just as easily have been the product of an incredibly vivid imagination. Elsa and I chose to believe that they were real and I did know for sure that they made one very sick little girl extremely happy. More importantly, they gave her a way of making sense of her suffering, of finding meaning in her illness. And, for that, I will be eternally grateful to whoever made these visits, whether real or imaginary, possible.

Then, out of the blue, things went terribly wrong for Elsa. One morning she awoke with a stabbing pain in her chest and a nasty cough. By the afternoon, she was running a high fever. Tests confirmed that Elsa had developed pneumonia and she was immediately transferred to intensive care again. Within two days, early one morning, she slipped into a coma, from which she was never to regain consciousness. A day later, despite the very best medical care, the little girl died.

The final part of Elsa's story is purely of my own imagining. Perhaps I needed a way to make sense of the terribly unfair way in which her short life had ended. Perhaps it was my way of offering a final tribute to a very sweet little girl, whom I had come to love very much. Either way, here is the final chapter in Elsa's story.

The night before Elsa slipped into the coma, the owl again appeared outside her window. *"I don't think I can climb out of the window,"* whispered Elsa to her visitor, *"I'm not strong enough any more."*

"Then we shall try another way of travelling," replied the owl. *"Close your eyes, Elsa, and imagine that you're back in the forest with all of your friends."* Elsa did as she was told and, after a very short period of darkness, she opened her eyes to find herself back in the forest glade, surrounded by the sylphs, with the Green Lady standing in front of her.

"Elsa, this is a very special celebration for you tonight," said the Lady. *"This is your farewell party because soon you will be going on an exciting journey to a new and different place, which is even more beautiful and lots more fun than this place."*

"More fun than here?" asked Elsa, *"That's not possible!"* But the Lady just smiled and took Elsa's hand to lead her into the dance. That night was the very best party that Elsa had ever been to. She danced until her cheeks were rosy and her hair surrounded her head in a wild, tangled halo. She danced until her legs finally collapsed and she tumbled onto the soft leaves underfoot and rolled around, giggling with joy. She ate and ate until she could eat no more and she played every game under the sun with her friends and with the Green Lady.

And then, finally, the Lady said to her, *"Elsa, it's time to leave now, little one. This party is over, but your new life is just about to begin."* And Elsa could tell by the little bubble of excitement running up her spine that the Lady was right. She knew that she was now ready for her next adventure, and so she bade all her friends farewell.

Then Elsa took the Lady's hand and together they walked between the two trees for a final time and out into a whole new world.

CHAPTER 14
THE GIANT GREY GHOSTS OF KNYSNA

It is virtually impossible to spend any length of time in the Garden Route without encountering the myths and legends surrounding the Knysna elephants. So, of course, I had heard the stories but I had never dared to hope that my own stay in Knysna would be graced by an actual personal encounter with these magnificent and mysterious creatures.

The Knysna elephants are a relic of the massive herds, comprising thousands of animals, which freely roamed the forests, fynbos and grasslands until they were driven almost to extinction by hunting. For a long time official sources insisted that there was only one elephant left, the so-called Matriarch, identifiable by her one broken tusk. Attempts to reintroduce elephants into the Knysna forests from elsewhere were a dismal failure. This meant, of course, that the Knysna elephants were now believed to be functionally extinct. However, more latterly, DNA analysis of dung samples has led scientists to believe that there are five cows, a few calves and possibly three bulls left, which represent the most southerly, free-ranging herd of elephants on the African continent. Some of these elephants have been caught on camera in recent years. These mysterious creatures have had to adapt their diet and to become silent and ghost-like; adept at moving almost invisibly so as to avoid human contact in order to ensure their continued survival.

This small and isolated herd of elephants secretly living deep within the ancient forests of Knysna has been immortalised in literature such as the famous book, *"Circles in a Forest"*, by author Dalene Matthee. Their existence is shrouded in mystery and is at the heart of much historic folklore of the area. Prior to the DNA evidence, many even doubted the existence of the herd altogether. It has been extremely difficult to track the elephants due to their legendary evasiveness, the density of the forest and the over sixty thousand hectares of open, unfenced area that they roam on the southern slopes of the forested Outeniqua mountains.

I had read extensively about the breathtakingly beautiful, so-called elephant hiking trails hidden within the Diepwalle forest, the last remaining remnants of the once extensive and magnificent tropical rainforest in which herds of elephants freely roamed without fear of humans. I knew that I had to find the time to explore these trails during my stay in Knysna.

One Saturday morning I awoke before dawn and drove for almost an hour up a steep, mountainous, dirt road, which winds for kilometres deep into the forest to eventually reach the Diepwalle Forestry station, from which the elephant hikes begin. I chose to do the longest of the three walks on offer - a nine kilometre hike through the densest moist forest of the area. By seven am I was already on the trail, my early lunch in a backpack. What a magnificent experience it turned out to be.

The inner sanctum of the forest is dense, featuring a wild profusion of an incredible diversity of flora, protected by the massive canopies of ancient trees meeting high above. The trail descends down steep riverbanks into a lush green world of moss, tree ferns, lichens and crystal-clear, sepia-toned streams. Bending to refill my water bottle at one such stream, I was alerted by a rustle in the undergrowth and found myself face-to-face with a startled bushbuck stag. After freezing for a moment, he darted away and I was delighted to catch a glimpse of his doe, rapidly following in his wake. Climbing the steep slope back out of the riverbed, I glanced up to catch sight of the brilliant red underside of the wings of the elusive and shy Knysna loerie. What a breathtaking vision, and unusually fortunate indeed. I couldn't help but think that this sighting could only be a good omen for the rest of my hike.

About halfway through my hike, I encountered a massive and magnificent ancient Yellowwood tree, several of its roots protruding high out of the ground to form a natural, secluded and protected seating arrangement. The Outeniqua Yellowwood can live for over a thousand years and has been known to grow up to sixty meters tall, although this specimen was a mere forty meters or so in height. I decided that this would be the perfect spot to enjoy my early lunch, as my breakfast had comprised only coffee and a few cookies, several hours earlier and I was absolutely ravenous.

I made myself comfortable, nestled between two enormous tree roots, with my back against the trunk of the tree and proceeded to enjoy my sandwiches and fruit. After lunch, I settled back against the tree trunk and glanced around, luxuriating in the breathtaking beauty of the golden sunlight gently filtering through tender green leaves and the wispy tendrils of mist swirling amongst the trees. I closed my eyes and breathed deeply of the atmosphere of this secret and beautiful place. Apart from the birdsong and the occasional rustling of the leaves, due to the hidden presence of forest creatures, it was remarkably peaceful and quiet. I felt decidedly sleepy, having worked till late on my book the previous evening and having made such an early start that morning. I felt myself slipping into a light doze, my head tipped back against the tree trunk. I dreamed of the mysterious elephants of the forest. Silent grey ghosts, slipping along secret pathways between ancient trees, bringing a message of hope; a message of life surviving, against all odds.

Some time later, I was awoken by a voice urgently whispering, *"Peter, wake up. Now!"* My eyes flew open as I distinctly heard the same voice cautioning, *"Be very quiet and don't move!"* From the corner of my eye I caught a bright flash of green light, but before I could even glance in that direction, I heard a crashing in the undergrowth. Turning in the direction of the noise, I gasped in amazement and terror and clapped a shaking hand over my mouth to prevent myself from crying out. Slowly, but inexorably wending her way along the path that passed directly in front of the tree in whose roots I was sheltering, was a massive, grey elephant! And then, my heart nearly stopped when I realised that she was not alone. Following the first elephant was another, and then, yet another! I counted five large female elephants and three calves moving in single file past my position. They moved surprisingly silently for such massive creatures. As they passed, one-by-one, not five meters away from me, I will admit that I had never been so terrified, or so completely exhilarated, in all my life. I sat silently, hardly breathing, every muscle in my body tensed. But, somehow, miraculously, they appeared oblivious to my presence. It was only the final elephant, the largest of the herd - a massive female with a broken tusk - that showed any awareness of my presence. She paused as she ambled past, lifted her trunk and delicately sniffed the air a meter or two away from my sweat-drenched face. She was so close that I could clearly see every deep crevasse in her craggy, leathery face and count each one of her long, grizzled, tangled eyelashes. And then she turned her head to look directly at me, her eyes deep wells of ancient wisdom, patience and acceptance. For a breathless moment of eternity we gazed at each other. Then she made a snorting noise, bobbed her massive head up-and-down a few times, and moved on. The elephants disappeared off the path and into the dense trees up ahead and, within a minute or two, it was as if they had never been there.

I sat for what seemed like hours, immobilized with shock and awe. Gradually my ego-mind took control and I started to think that perhaps I had dreamt or imagined the entire experience. After all, I had been dozing. Perhaps the whole experience had just been some sort of lucid dream, brought on by my surroundings and by my recent preoccupation with the legends of the Knysna elephants. My terrified mind rushed to reassure me that it simply wasn't possible to have experienced what I thought I had experienced. Eventually I dragged my stiff and painful body into an upright position, staggered to my feet and resumed my hike, now thoroughly convinced that I had indeed imagined the entire event.

But then, just ten metres or so from the Yellowwood tree where I had enjoyed my lunch, I was presented with incontrovertible proof. A massive pile of dung... still gently steaming in the cool forest air.

CHAPTER 15
ALL IS ONE

As my story-collecting sabbatical in Knysna drew to a close, I found myself with far more questions than answers. Why had so many people experienced transformative events in the forests of this region? Who, or what, were people connecting with in the forest? What mysterious secrets were hidden here? Most importantly, who was this Green Lady and how was she related to all those to whom she chose to reveal herself?

I had met so many interesting people and documented so many fascinating stories that I felt a very strong connection with the town and its people. It had started to feel as if I belonged here in this beautiful place and I knew that I would be leaving a large part of myself behind when I departed within the next few days. On my many hikes in the area, I had felt an increasing connection to, and love of, the beautiful forests and natural indigenous vegetation. So, during my final week, I decided to go for one last hike in the forest to clear my mind and to say goodbye to the mysterious and wonderful forests of Knysna.

Stepping out onto the footpath into the forest, I picked up my pace and gradually became aware of my body working, my muscles stretching, my breathing deepening; blood rushing to my feet and legs as I moved up the incline. I found myself gradually releasing the accumulated stress of the day, as the multitude of small concerns and questions occupying my mind diminished with every deep breath that I took. Slowly the incessant chattering of my mind quietened and I began to take notice of the incredible beauty of my surroundings.

Slowing down my pace, I started absorbing the essence of the forest through all of my senses, through the very pores of my skin, and gradually my perception of the forest began to change, increasing in energy, in vitality, taking on the appearance of a stage or movie set, becoming simply too intense in its being-ness, simply too perfect to be real. The almost psychedelic colours, the myriad textures, the richness of smells; the placement of every tiny twig and stone seemed simply too perfect to have happened by chance. It became impossible for me to believe that there wasn't an incredible design, some awesome intelligence behind it all. As I tiptoed with reverence through massive tree cathedrals and gazed with awe upon delicate green lace-light filtering through living stained glass windows, I became convinced that I was in the presence of a collective intelligence - a spirit of the forest. Well could I believe the many stories I had been told of the Lady of the forest. Sitting down beside a small waterfall, cascading through delicate, luminous greenery into a pool below, I breathed deeply in gratitude and appreciation.

Suddenly a greenish glow appeared, and from behind a dense tangle of large tree ferns a beautiful woman emerged and walked toward me. Her skin was pale green and subtly glowing, as if lit from within, and her wild tangle of waist-length, dark green hair was threaded through with small white flowers and delicate ferny fronds. She wore no conventional garments but her lithe body radiated such a beautiful light that she appeared to be fully clothed. I jumped to my feet, my heart pounding in fear and excitement as I realised that finally I too would be meeting the Lady of whom I had heard so many tales. She smiled at me so sweetly that I was sure that she could read my thoughts and I felt engulfed in deep, calm warmth and acceptance.

"Who are you really?" I asked, *"And where have you come from?"*

"I am the Deva of the forest", she replied, *"And I have been here all along! You are simply able to see me now because of your relaxed, meditative state of deep gratitude and appreciation. I often watch over you on your walks in the forest and I believe that you have reached a place of readiness to be shown some wonderful things that will increase your understanding of the forest and of your relationship to it."* So saying, the beautiful woman walked up to me and placed her cool, soft hands gently over my eyes.

"What are you doing?" I asked, rather bemused by this unexpected turn of events.

"Simply removing the veil from your sight. Behold what lies before you!" she exclaimed as she removed her hands from my face.

Opening my eyes, I gasped in delight to see a magical fairyland of wonder. The light shining through the trees had taken on a liquid golden hue, which reflected off the shimmering wings of a myriad tiny, dancing creatures of sparkling coloured light that enchanted the air around us. *"What on earth...?"* I exclaimed in wonderment, suddenly realizing that I was finally seeing some of the beings who had so delighted my little sick friend, Elsa.

"They are sylphs; air spirits which tend to the growth of trees, plants and flowers. Sylphs are one class of elemental beings, all of which have the job of transforming thought-forms into physical forms."

"But, how do they do that?" I asked in amazement.

"It may be a little difficult for you to understand, but basically sylphs channel etheric energies into producing the physical forms of plants, using the blueprints supplied by the Devas, to whom they report."

Seeing a bright flash of light out of the corner of my eye, I turned to catch a brief glimpse of a small, fiery, lizard-like creature darting into the undergrowth next to a fallen tree stump. *"What was that?"* I asked my beautiful guide.

"That was a salamander – a fire spirit. Their job is the transformation of matter from one form to another. In this particular case, the rotting tree trunk and plant matter is transformed by the salamander into nutrients that support the growth of new plants. Absolutely everything is recycled in the forest, you know! Forest salamanders are generally quite small, but the salamanders attending volcanoes, lightning or other large sources of transformative energy can be massive. It is always very important to have the highest intent when lighting a fire, because salamanders are just like mischievous children and can cause great harm if your intent is not pure."

"What are these elemental beings made of; surely not flesh-and-blood?" I asked, beginning to really enjoy this unique experience.

"Definitely not flesh-and-blood!" she laughed. *"Each different type of elemental being is made of the etheric substance that is unique and specific to their particular element. The four elements being, of course, earth, air, fire and water. Although the elementals are not immortal, they do live for many hundreds of years, carrying out their specific functions before they, once again, revert back to the etheric substance from which they were initially formed. Now, if you look over at that waterfall, you will see a nymph, which is a type of undine - water elementals who work with the vital*

essences and liquids of plants and animals." Looking at the waterfall I saw a brilliant being of pale blue light which briefly flickered in greeting and then disappeared beneath the water.

"But... these beings are the stuff of myths and legends! I never realised that they actually existed! How is it that humans cannot usually perceive them?" I asked the Deva.

"In ancient times humans actually did perceive the elementals to a far greater degree that you currently do; hence the myths and legends. However, in more modern times, due to the toxic wastes of industrialisation and the destruction of vast tracts of previously unspoilt land, many of the elementals have withdrawn into seclusion or have left entirely. As a result of the ascendance of the human ego and mind, natural human receptivity has almost shut down, and the elementals have become invisible to just about everyone. However, children will often perceive them, as will people who are in a receptive state, such as you are in today," she answered.

Pointing to a pile of rocks beside the waterfall, where I could see a small, brown creature steadily moving along the surface of the rocks, she said, *"Over there you can see an Earth spirit. They are concerned with the minerals in rocks and soils, which, you will be surprised to know, are also living entities. They perform an important nutrient function in the bodies of all living things. Without minerals the plants and animals could not survive."*

The Deva turned to face me again and said, *"In addition to the elementals I have shown you, and countless others besides, you should also be aware that your pets, and even your own body, have associated elemental spirits. If you work together with these elementals, you can ensure the continued health and well-being of yourself and that of your* animal companions. Simply return to this relaxed, meditative state and allow yourself to feel gratitude, deep within your heart. Then ask the specific elemental to assist you in your quest for health, balance and well-being. It is their duty and their greatest pleasure to assist you."

"But, having encountered all these different elementals, I'm wondering exactly who YOU are," I said.

The Deva smiled gently at me and replied, "*The entire forest, including all the plants, animals, minerals, micro-organisms, the air, the water, absolutely everything, is a massive co-creative, living entity. I am the energy essence of that entity and I am responsible for the health and well-being thereof. It is with me that you communicate when you experience yourself in communication with the forest.*"

After allowing me a few moments to internalise this piece of information, the Deva continued, "*Now I would like to guide you in your quest toward better understanding of the forest. I am well aware of the questions that you have been asking yourself in this regard and today I'm going to help you to find a few answers. Firstly, I want you to realise that when you walk in the forest you are actually engaged in a conversation with the forest on many different levels. On the chemical level, you are breathing in oxygen and a multitude of microscopic compounds produced by the plants, animals and micro-organisms that live in the forest and, in return, they are taking up the carbon dioxide that you breathe out, as well as obtaining vital information about you, your diet, your stresses, your attitudes and many, many other bits of information from the molecules that you breathe out. This chemical conversation changes both you and the forest. I think you've noticed how you become calmer and more relaxed when walking in the forest?*" I nodded my assent and the Deva continued, "*Of course you are also communicating on an emotional and spiritual level with the forest. Your feelings of love and gratitude literally feed the forest, as they provide vital energy to the elementals to do their work of growing plants and animals. Your loving intent is made manifest by these spirit workers.*"

"*But... that's just incredible!*" I expostulated. "*That means that I truly am connected to the forest in many different ways. I have so often felt this connection but always thought that it was only my own imagination!*"

The Deva slowly smiled, as if she had been waiting for me to reach this very conclusion. She leaned over and took my hand. "*I'm about to show you how very deep that connection really is,*" she said. "*Just relax and don't resist as I take you on a little journey into the very heart of matter.*"

So saying, she pulled me to my feet and then suddenly the golden light surrounding us began twisting and swirling in a crazy spiral of energy and we were sucked into the spiral, moving at breathtaking speeds in a dizzying rush of colour, light and sound. As I gradually became accustomed to the sensations, her voice sounded in my mind, "*We are now travelling inward towards the very smallest units of matter. Along the way I'll point out some sights. On your right you will see us passing an amoeba.*" I barely had time to take in the sight of the massive, single-celled monster waving its tentacles at us before we rushed past a tubular *E. coli* bacterium and, further in, a virus, looking just like a space exploration unit. And then, we were rushing past molecules and atoms and electrons and, a long, long way in, we reached the nucleus of an atom and sub-atomic particles. My head was spinning as we finally reached the smallest sub-atomic particles. The Deva explained to me that these were not even particles at all, but simply potentialities that popped in-and-out of existence all the time. It was mind-boggling to realise that our entire physical world was made up of stuff that didn't actually exist! This reality truly was an illusion, as the mystics had always asserted it to be. But stranger sights were yet to be experienced.

Our mad headlong rush ended abruptly and I looked around to find myself in a strange ocean of shimmering energy, brimming with potentiality. *"Where are we now?"* I asked the Deva in a hushed voice.

"This is the zero-point energy field," she whispered back. *"At this level, all is truly One."* As I looked around, the truth of what she was saying became clear to me. The infinite energy field permeated and inter-penetrated everything I saw. Looking down at my own body, I could see that the energy outside of my body was exactly the same as the energy inside of my body. Energy moved freely through my body; in fact my body was simply made of the same energy as everything else. I certainly didn't end where my skin ended. Looking at the Deva in confusion, I could see that she too was a constantly moving, ever-changing cloud of energy. The thought occurred to me that if the Deva represented the forest, and if both she and I were made up of the same energy, then the forest and I were truly One being. My mind struggled to contain that thought and I reached out to the Deva for assistance in understanding.

"But... then... what am I?" I asked, completely overwhelmed by the mystery and the magic of what I was experiencing.

"There are many ways of describing what you are," she replied, *"It all depends upon your viewing point or your perspective when you ask the question. Your body, your*

personality construct, your mind; these are all like an eddy in the stream of energy. The energy stream constantly moves and changes and, as you have observed, freely flows through you, but you are a standing pattern in the energy stream for a few brief moments. However, if you take a higher view, then you could be described as a perspective in the stream of consciousness that makes up all that is. There are infinite perspectives, but from the highest perspective of all, you, me, the forest, the Earth and all of her inhabitants, the planets, stars, galaxies, the entire Universe and beyond... are all One. It is all an expression of God. You, my dear friend, are an expression of God."

With a sudden flash of insight, I realised that we humans are labouring under the mistaken illusion that we are separate and alone. And yet we desperately yearn for our natural state of unity and connection. So we chase money, careers, possessions, sex, love, addictions; anything that we hope will bring us, even fleetingly, the experience of One-ness that we desire. Of course, the grand irony is that there is no way we can not be One, for this is our true nature; it is the true nature of All That Is.

The magnificent wonder of everything I had learnt and experienced permeated my being and my consciousness, and I felt my boundaries gradually begin to disintegrate as my perspective of myself as a separate entity slowly disappeared and I gratefully sank into the infinite wonder of BE-ing... One...

Eons later I awoke to the familiar illusion of my own separateness and found myself lying on a soft pile of dead leaves at the side of the waterfall; the forest having been returned to its own familiar, but more mundane beauty. However, as I turned to leave, a brief flash of green light flashed between the trees and I smiled at the joyful realisation that, within my own being, I now held the sure knowledge of my connection to my beloved forest. But, most of all, my connection to All That Is.

I also knew, with absolute certainty, that just as so many had before me, I would very shortly be returning to this place, never to leave again. I just had no idea of how I was going to make that happen

Epilogue

My long-awaited and eagerly anticipated meeting with the Green Lady had indeed been a massively transformative experience for me. I found myself completely convinced that she indeed existed, just as had all the people whose stories I had documented been convinced. I was of the opinion that anyone who spent any time at all in the forests would be forever changed.

As I put the finishing touches to my stories in the final days before my time in Knysna would draw to an end, the realization gradually began to dawn on me that I would no longer be able to return to my previous life. My experiences in this beautiful part of the world had irrevocably changed me and it was no longer possible to even contemplate a city life and a career in journalism. But, what would I do with my life, then? Was it possible that I could find a way to live in Knysna, close to the forests that had so transformed my perspective on life?

On my final day in Knysna, I took a short walk to bid the forests farewell. As I sat on a large stone in the middle of a mountain stream, surrounded by lush green tree ferns and protected by the tree canopy high above, I made a pledge to myself that I would indeed return to live in Knysna, no matter what it would take. I had made my choice. And it was a choice about love and connection and an open heart. It was a choice about connecting with my most authentic self and trusting what I found there instead of accepting the limited perspective of my ego-mind.

And, indeed, it seems that when we make a choice from the heart, the entire universe conspires to make it happen in the most unexpected ways. I had barely arrived back in Cape Town when I received a phone call from Helena Kroukamp, the journalist with whom I had worked on crowdfunding Elsa's treatment. Helena told me that her German boyfriend had finally asked her to marry him and that she would be moving to Germany within the next few months to live with him there. She asked me whether I would be interested in taking over her regular columns in various newspapers and magazines in the region. She said that she would also be willing to introduce me, with a personal recommendation, to all of her contacts in case I was interested in writing the odd article or opinion piece for extra cash. The income would be a fraction of what I had earned in Cape Town and it was a career dead-end, but I was elated. In addition, Helena told me that she would put in a good word for me with her landlord and that, if I wanted it, her small, extremely inexpensive apartment would become available at the beginning of the following month.

And so it was that I found myself back in Knysna, only two months after leaving, with a job, a home and plenty of time and energy left at the end of each day to continue pursuing my passion for writing. The very next day I planned a hike in the forest. I was hoping to meet with the Green Lady to thank her for all that she had done for me. What transpired next is the topic of another book...

The
End

Thank you for reading my book. I really loved writing it! If you enjoyed reading it, won't you please take a moment to leave me a review at your favourite retailer?
- Lisa Picard

ABOUT THE AUTHOR

I am an ex-corporate warrior who, like so many of the characters in my book, *The Green Lady*, had a transformative experience in the forests of Knysna several years ago. I recorded a diary of my experience, including my mystical moment and the process of moving to the forests and constructing my own home, with my partner, Arn. You are invited to read all about it on my website at: thegreenlady.zingdad.com/about/diary-from-ego-to-heart.html

This life-altering experience was the catalyst that eventually led to my leaving my city life and corporate job and moving to a remote smallholding in the Outeniqua Mountains of South Africa's Garden Route. My life partner, fellow author and spiritual healer, Arn Allingham, and I built our off-the-grid home with our own hands. As of 2010, we have been enjoying a simple, but deeply connected, life here on the border of the beautiful indigenous forest. It is my greatest joy and the expression of my most authentic self to share my love and appreciation of the forests with others through my writing.

Connect with me:
Visit my website at thegreenlady.zingdad.com
Follow my blog thegreenlady.zingdad.com/blog
Visit my Facebook page at facebook.com/thegreenladybook

You can read on my website about my personal journey from ego to heart in the diary that I wrote documenting my transition from my city life to the life that I currently lead.

Additional writings, including a few short stories, can also be found on my website.

Many of the themes in *The Green Lady* are explored at far greater depth in the book, *The Ascension Papers*, written by my life partner, Arn (Zingdad) Allingham. This transformative and deeply healing e-book is available for free from his website. Should you prefer a paperback book, then you can also order one off Arn's website. The link is:
zingdad.com/books/the-ascension-papers-book-1

Besides being an author, Arn is also a talented healer and facilitator. If you are interested in healing your pain or in finding your own most authentic expression of self, then I invite you to visit Arn's website at zingdad.com, to find out more about his **Soul Re-integration** healing modality and his self-study workbooks, *"Create Yourself, Create Your Life"* and the life-changing *"Dreamer Awake!"* seminar series.

Should you be interested in combining a visit to the magnificent Knysna forests with powerful spiritual healing, then check out Arn's **African Spiritual Safaris** on zingdad.com

You too may possibly meet the Green Lady for yourself!

Q&A WITH LISA PICARD, AUTHOR OF THE GREEN LADY

Is *The Green Lady* written for adults or for children?
The book is written for children of all ages who sense and appreciate the deep mystery and wonder of the forests.

What was your inspiration for this book?
The magnificent beauty of the forests of the Garden Route; but also forests that I have visited all over the world. There is some incredible connection, a sense of peace and indescribable elation, that I feel whenever I am in the forest. This was my inspiration.

It is often said that all novels are autobiographical. Is this the case for *The Green Lady*?
The book is set in the Garden Route of South Africa, and mostly in the town of Knysna, which is the closest town to where I live. So, many of the places I mention in the book are real. However, the characters and events are all purely fictional, although, like most authors, I am often inspired by people I have met or experiences I have had.

I have included several of the themes of my life and personal development during the past five years or so in *The Green Lady*. Such themes include: connecting with the heart, trusting your own inner guidance and the search for meaning and purpose in life. Also, many of the characters represent different aspects of my personality and of my passions. For example, the passion of Benjamin Leigh in the story, **Expression of Your Authentic Self**, for alien vegetation management is also a reflection of one of my own passions. The story of Greg and Sandi in **Follow Your Heart** reflects a part of the journey of my partner and myself in building our own off-the-grid home, even though we did use a more conventional building method than the characters chose to use. The peak experience of Ken in the story of the same name and also of a few of the other characters is based upon such an experience that I personally had, which ultimately led to my own move to Knysna. So, yes, I suppose that this book is, to some extent, autobiographical in nature.

Have you ever met the Green Lady yourself?
I think that a little part of me IS actually the Green Lady! When I am in the forest and experiencing that connection I mentioned before, I am often convinced that I am being observed by some greater entity. It often feels to me as if the forest is communicating with me on a very deep level and I draw such energy and inspiration from the place that... how can there not be a Green Lady!

Like many of the characters in the book, you too have moved from the city to the small town of Knysna. Tell your readers a bit about your journey.
I was a boardroom warrior in a large, multinational corporate when I had a transformative experience in the Knysna area. You can read more about my experience in my diary that is available on my website at
thegreenlady.zingdad.com/about/diary-from-ego-to-heart.html

My life partner and I, like several of the characters in my stories in *The Green Lady*, liquidated our assets and moved to a small community, high up in the Outeniqua Mountains and bordering on the indigenous forest, where we built, mostly with our own hands, an off-the-grid home. This is where we still live and where I continue to write.

What is so special about Knysna and the surrounding forests?
It is a magical, exquisitely beautiful place. I've travelled extensively all over the world but this place remains my home and the only place I want to be. Come for a visit and see for yourself!

Will there be further Green Lady books?
My lovely green muse has, once again, tapped me on the shoulder! I am currently working on the sequel to *The Green Lady*, called *The Story of the Green Lady*. In this book, the Green Lady shares her own personal story with Peter Allen.

Who is the Green Lady really? Where did she come from? What is her purpose in the world? What message does she have to share with us?

You can find the answers to these questions and many others in my new book. An excerpt from *The Story of the Green Lady* can be found in the pages following this section

Why did you decide to write a book?
I've always written, as a way of working things out in my own mind, as an expression of my inner-self or just for fun. But this book asked me to write it and so I had to oblige.

You appear to be very passionate about conservation. Tell your readers a bit more about that.
I am extremely passionate about conserving and protecting this perfect place. By contributing my time and energy to this goal, I find my connection to the forests ever deepening and the benefits that I reap far outweigh the energy expenditure.

What is the one take-home message you'd like to leave your readers with?
There is always magic and beauty and enchantment... just a heartbeat away; if you would but choose to see it.

Excerpt from: The Story of the Green Lady

On a freezing cold and wet winter's Saturday afternoon I arrived in the peaceful coastal town of Knysna, with all of my worldly possessions piled high in the back of a small pick-up truck I had loaned from a long-suffering friend. As I drove along the deserted main road, I was suddenly filled with misgiving, remembering the vibrant, busy roads of Cape Town, which I had so recently departed. I wondered whether I was cut out for the life in a quiet town that had none of the distractions I was so accustomed to enjoying as a city dweller. There wasn't even a movie house in this one-horse town, for goodness sake! And definitely no sign of stylish coffee shops, award-winning restaurants or glitzy clubs. I had always been a city dweller, but there was no turning back now, as my bridges were well-and-truly burnt, I mused, easing the truck into the parking area of the modest apartment building in which I would be living for the foreseeable future. At least there was plenty of parking - something which no city dweller will ever take for granted.

An hour later the pick-up was emptied of my meagre belongings, the bulk of which now resided in the middle of my sitting room inside of a pathetic pile of soggy cardboard boxes. Hanging up my dripping raincoat in the shower, its mouldy, drooping curtain adorned with seventies-style mustard-coloured swirls, I was finding it increasingly difficult to keep my spirits up. What on Earth had I been thinking of to resign from my lucrative job as a journalist at a top Cape Town daily newspaper? How could I possibly have exchanged my comfortable, stylish city house for this tiny, miserable apartment?

Mentally giving myself a shake and yanking myself back from the temptation of a lengthy wallow in a mire of self-pity, I reminded myself that this had been my choice. I had willingly given up my career and my city life. For better or for worse, I had decided that this was my dream and I was determined to make the most of it.

Grabbing a beer from the cooler box on the floor, I threw myself down onto a pile of cushions on the futon, which would have to fulfil the dual function of a bed and a couch in my new Spartan living quarters. Cracking open the can and taking a long, cool swig, I mentally reviewed the events that had resulted in my current situation.

Ten months earlier, my long-term girlfriend, Clare, had left me, due to our irreconcilable visions for our shared future. Hers included marriage and children and mine... well I was actually unsure of exactly what I had wanted at the time. My previously cherished job, as a well-regarded journalist of some fifteen years, was no longer satisfying to me and I had been ready for a change. A series of chance encounters led to my taking a six-month sabbatical in Knysna. During my sabbatical I spent my time collecting stories of super-natural and transformative encounters in the forests of the region. I had the idea of writing these up for a book. My time spent in Knysna culminated in a personal encounter with the mysterious Green Lady of the forest, which proved to be transformative for me as well. Upon my return to Cape Town, I resigned from my job and set about packing up my life to move back to Knysna for good. I decided that I would support myself working as a free-lance journalist, at a fraction of the salary I had previously earned. But my real work would be to finalise the writing of my first book, get it published and hopefully begin work on the following book.

Returning from my little trip down memory lane, I clicked my tongue in self-disgust. My plans now appeared hopelessly optimistic and over-ambitious. What did I know about writing and publishing a book? And who could possibly be interested in the topic I had chosen? That seductive self-pity wallow beckoned me yet again.

Pushing myself up from my prone position and staggering to my feet, clutching my aching back, I threw my empty beer can at the wall in disgust. I knew that I would get nothing done in my current mood and so I decided to take myself off to the local pub for a few drinks, a meal and hopefully some congenial company to lift myself out of my funk.

In the pub I fortuitously encountered Ken Brady, a marine biologist working in Knysna whose story I had included in my first book. By the time we had consumed a burger each and had downed a few beers, I was feeling considerably more positive about my situation. I returned to my apartment to start unpacking my few belongings in an attempt to create a slightly more homely environment, hopefully more conducive to creativity.

The following morning I awoke in a brilliant beam of sunlight shining through the curtain-less windows. Things seemed much more positive than they had on the previous day. I'd made it! Here I was in Knysna, about to commence my new life, in which I would follow my heart towards expressing myself as grandly as I could. What was there to feel low about?

After a quick breakfast of cereal, I gathered up the flattened cardboard boxes, which I took to the recycling depot, and then bought a prepared sandwich and a few granola bars and got into the truck to drive up the mountain to one of my favourite forest hikes. After all, I reasoned, it was Sunday and I deserved to have some time off to recover from my move.

My spirits lifted even further as I stepped onto the trail. The forest was exquisite after the rain, with droplets sparkling on each newly-washed, intensely bright-green leaf. My nostrils welcomed as an old friend the aromas of humus-rich, moist, fertile soil. I found myself humming a jaunty little tune as I stretched my pace, breathing deeply of the healing energies of this most lovely of places.

Within a couple of hours I had reached the massive ancient Yellowwood tree in whose roots I had sheltered during my dream-like encounter with the mysterious Knysna elephants earlier that year. Placing my raincoat on the ground to protect my clothing from the damp forest floor, I settled down amongst the roots and enjoyed my picnic. Afterwards, I simply relaxed, basking in the atmosphere of the place. I remembered what the Green Lady had told me about opening my heart and allowing myself to feel love and gratitude for the forest, and so this is exactly what I did.

Within a few minutes, the light illuminating the pale-green leaves began to deepen to a rich, golden hue. The varied colours and textures of the trees and plants, moss, fungi and lichen began to intensify and I became acutely aware of the magnificent density of life surrounding me. The crickets, frogs and songbirds, the rustling of the undergrowth as small creatures visited this magical place and the chattering of the canopy above as the breeze caressed the trees, all contributed to a delightful, harmonious symphony of vibrant life.

Briefly, there was silence as the forest held its breath in a moment of anticipation. Someone was coming...

And then, suddenly, there she was, gliding across the forest floor towards me - her hands outstretched in welcome, her beautiful face glowing with gentle green light and her eyes twinkling in a smile.

"Peter, you have returned home at last," she said, touching my arm with her fingertips. I was suffused with joy as I realised that her words were true and that I had, indeed, returned to my spiritual home. I scrambled to my feet with a delightful sense of anticipation. Something wonderful was about to happen!

"I didn't know that I was coming home. I've only just realised that... this very minute, as you said the words," I babbled, feeling overwhelmed with joy. The Green Lady giggled and said,

"Peter, you should know by now that the forest, lovely as it is, is not what I was referring to! You have returned home to yourself; to your own heart. You have begun to follow your heart, to trust in your own authority and your own knowing rather than seeking affirmation and direction from outside of yourself. This is the very first step on your journey towards finding and expressing your most authentic self. And you are rightly feeling suffused with joy, because this is simply the most joy-filled journey you will ever undertake. The journey to Self." The Green Lady gracefully sank down onto a moss-covered log and indicated that I too should sit. Then she said, *"Peter, I have been following your progress with great interest and I know that your first book will be cherished by many. But, more importantly, you have contributed towards an increase in consciousness in the world by writing it. Now, I know that there is still some work to be done in finalising the book and in*

making it available for people to read and, of course, this work must progress. But, at the same time, you need to start getting into the right frame of mind to write your next book."

"My next book? But... but, I have no plans at the moment to do such a thing. I'm feeling completely intimidated by the huge amount of work required to finish the first book! And, besides, I have absolutely no ideas or inspiration for another book right now!" I expostulated, suddenly feeling overwhelmed. The Green Lady leaned over and placed her hand on my chest, over my heart, and the anxiety left me, to be replaced by a feeling of calm centeredness.

"Peter, it's natural to feel a bit daunted by all of this change. But that should not stop you doing what your heart calls you to do. Your next book is waiting in the wings and, as for inspiration...well, that's what I'm here for," a bright, tinkling little laugh that both warmed and opened my heart trilled from her throat.

"Your first book shared the stories of people who had encountered me. Your next book will share my own stories; the stories of how I became the Green Lady and what that means," she said.

"Oh, but I would love to write those stories," I gasped with excitement. "In fact, I can't think of any other stories that I would rather write at this point!"

"And that, my dear friend, is a sure sign that you are on your path; that you are starting to express your most authentic self," she smiled. "Follow the joy, follow the excitement, follow the fascination and the curiosity and they will lead you to ever greater and greater expressions of your most authentic self. For now, it will be the writing of The Story of the Green Lady, but, in future, who knows where your joy will lead you!

But let's stay focused for now on the next step. So, what I propose is this: you will come to this place in the forest once a week, on a Sunday afternoon, and we will spend an hour or two together. I will tell you the stories of the many lives I have experienced and how these lives have led to my becoming the being you see before you. These will be thrilling stories of seekers and soldiers, of priests and shamans, of aliens and of ordinary human beings. Stories of adventure and discovery but, ultimately, the story of ever-deepening understanding and appreciation of the Self. In short, Peter, it is the story of Life itself. And, in the receiving and the writing of my story, you will find yourself on your own journey of discovery of your most magnificent and most authentic Self. You will be writing your own story too."

"But, this sounds simply wonderful," I gasped, *"I can't wait to begin!"*

"Then, I will next see you in a week's time," she smiled as she stood up, raised her hand in greeting and then drifted away between the trees.

I sat for several minutes longer, relishing the excitement of the knowledge of what lay ahead. My new life truly was about to begin...

To continue following The Story of The Green Lady, please visit thegreenlady.zingdad.com

At the time of writing this work was still in progress. If it is not yet published, please register for the author's free newsletter, featuring exciting developments from the world of the Green Lady, including new publication dates. Sign up right now at: <u>thegreenlady.zingdad.com/newsletter.html</u>

www.ingramcontent.com/pod-product-compliance
Lightning Source LLC
Chambersburg PA
CBHW070454260626
47161CB00004B/1298